LETTERS FROM LLANABER

Global politics seen through life in this strange tiny village in West Wales

A COLLECTION OF THE FIRST 50 NEWSLETTERS
WRITTEN BY THE LLANABER PARISH FOREIGN SECRETARY

AN INTRODUCTION TO LLANABER:

Llanaber is a tiny village by the seaside in West Wales with its own micro-climate (perpetual fog), village attractions (a variety of small shops set around a massive sink hole in the main street), neighboring villages (Druidellau, Spanibont and Bogbourne) and political shenanigans worthy of Capitol Hill itself.

Llanaber is a microcosm of the US. As with Lorenz' 'butterfly effect' what happens in the US effects Llanaber, especially as the mad old bat that runs the parish council,
Mrs. Dorothy 'Binky' Trim, will plagiarize even the craziest Trump idea.

Village life is documented in the village 'letter' written by the parish council's Foreign Secretary, David Smith. The characters and events in the village may seem bizarre beyond belief but take a closer look. Are they really that different to what's happening in 'the real world?'

Published by Torn Wires Limited Liability Company

admin@tornwires.com

tornwires.com

This book is David Smith's fourteenth.
Find out about his other bestsellers and his next project
at www.davidsmithbooks.co.uk

****

A dedication: Who else would I dedicate this book to but the
best person I've ever met, my wonderful wife and best pal,
Ally.

****

Acknowledgements: My special thanks to Moe Flake of 'The Flake News' for all his support with this project and for his permission to use the images that he added to my articles. Also, my thanks to Wes Cooper from Torn Wires for his help and encouragement.

Other books by David Smith:

One Bad Penny
One Bad Gig
Another Bad Gig
Seeds of Freedom
The Seed Cloud
Guests of Horror
The Last Train Home
Peek-A-Boo

Whistleblower
Whistleblower (The Screenplays)
Retribution
JAM (Just About Managing)
Ten Tense Tales

Contents

LLANABER - NEW FOREIGN SECRETARY APPOINTED

Our little village on the West coast of Wales elected a new council leader last year, Mrs. Dorothy 'Binky' Trim. She owns the sweet shop in the village. I don't like to speak unpleasantly about anyone but she's a bit hard faced. Ever since we got running water into nearly all the houses in the village last year, she has visions of taking her place on the world stage.

At the Llanaber parish council meeting last night I had the misfortune to suddenly be taken short. (I blame the wife's leek soup. She put something she laughingly calls thunder-dust in it to thicken it up). Mrs. T was in the middle of another one of her long-winded speeches about cutbacks when the rumbling started. I only just made it in time.

The point I'm coming to is when I returned somewhat exhausted from the restroom I found to my consternation that there'd been a vote in my absence, the upshot of which is that I've been given the job for the foreseeable future of Parish Foreign Secretary responsible for defense, immigration, and other foreign affairs. As such I produce a weekly report on what's happening in the world and how whatever's going on impinges on our quiet little village. I admit we can be a little parochial in Llanaber and there's a need to keep abreast, but really? I've been told to simplify the bulletins so it can be added into the parish newsletter. Mrs. T said my duties start with immediate effect, so here goes.

What Donald Trump did recently:

For those in the village that have never heard of him he's the President (Boss) of America. This week there's been a lot of fuss about him welching on something called the joint comprehensive plan of action. I think this is either to do with stuff they smoke over there or Iran, probably the latter. Iran has been saving up for a nuclear bomb and Mr. Obama (the old boss) had been chipping in. Iran has a lot of Mullahs and Mr. Trump has a thing against them. There's one in America called Robert he particularly dislikes.

According to Mr. Trump the Iranians can't be trusted. And, because he's a man of his word, he doesn't want to deal with people that can't be trusted. So, he's unilaterally pulling out of the legally binding agreement signed by the US. There's someone who lives next door to Iran called Benjamin Netanyahu who tipped off Mr. Trump that the Mullahs were stockpiling water in a mountain – I think you can't really blame them for that. They live in a desert. Unless a few more people chip in to take up the slack, the poor Iranians won't be able to afford their bomb. But Mr. Trump will have nothing to do with people that lie.

There's been a bit of a kerfuffle lately about Mr. Trump's ex-girlfriend, Stormy Daniels. I think last year he lent her some money for Hush Puppies but his lawyer paid it, not him. There's some confusion as to who paid who what and when.

The outcome is Mrs. Trump's embarrassed that her husband has been lending money without charging interest, and I think wants to take the shoes off Mrs. Daniels. I'm sure there's more to this story than meets the eye. There's a bloke called Giuliani (who looks like the consiglieri in that first Godfather film). I can't fathom out what he's got to do with it but he's put his ten pen'orth in saying $130,000 is not that much for a pair of shoes (what planet is he from?). Anyway, I'm sure they'll all sort it out amicably between them and Stormy can keep her shoes.

That's enough for this issue. I'll be sending another one out next week. Cheerio!

US SPAT WITH IRAN MAY CAUSE TRADE HAVOC IN LLANABER

Mrs. T's been throwing her weight about again at the parish meeting. As she's worked in the village sweet shop since she was a toddler, she has a considerable amount to throw about as well!

Llanaber has its own microclimate. This time of year, we get four weeks of bad weather before winter sets in. But with this climate change the Americans are so keen on, the perpetual fog lifted for an hour last night. That meant the village could receive TV signal, and, guess what? Mrs. T just happened to be watching the box having her bedtime cup of cocoa at the time. The news was on. There was an article about Donald Trump. I gather from her rant in the council meeting that Mr. Trump is going to impose secondary sanctions on people that trade with Iran, and that has got her worried sick.

Why?

Turkish Delight.

Mrs. T is convinced her sweets supplier buys this from Iran, and it's a big seller in her shop. She's worried sick Donald Trump will not only cut off her supply but will stop her selling sweets to American tourists (we had seven last year and they're big spenders!). I told her not to be an old worry guts. I said, 'The clue's in the title – *Turkish* Delight!' All her sweets are supplied from 'Turkish Sweet and Savory Supplies Ltd.' and they're based in Aberystwyth. What's more, I know for a fact they get their Turkish Delight from North Korea.

How do I know?

I was in Mrs. T's shop when she opened a box and this little Korean chap jumped out shouting, 'Death to America!' He was tiny. We think he fell in the box at the factory and couldn't get out. Mrs. T happened to be in one of her rare good moods that day so she gave him political asylum and got him a job in the village bakery. His little hands are the perfect size for making the holes in the donuts.

Anyway, the upshot is that she's insisted that I write a letter to Mr. Trump to ask if he'll make 'Nanny Trim's Sweets 'N' Stuff' a special case, exempt from secondary sanctions. Also, I have to add a copy to the parish newsletter to let the village know what an important job we're doing protecting our economy from the disruption caused by international affairs.

So, here goes.

"Dear Mr. President,

I know you must be busy, what with being the boss of America, running your hotel and catering businesses, and having all those girlfriends to take out, but can I ask a favor? It's about your spat with Iran. I know you're not seeing eye-to-eye with them at the moment and you've stopped chipping in towards their bomb. But in fairness they're nice people. I saw on the news they'd started burning US flags. They were burning loads of them, in their parliament and in the streets. Sales of Stars and Stripes flags must be going through the roof over there! So they are doing their bit to try and help your economy. Their hearts are in the right place.

I saw recently you'd had a spat with that little fat lad who runs North Korea. But I see you've changed your mind about him. Was it because he finally came out? To be honest it surprised me when I saw him on the news holding hands with that other Korean chap. Still, it's understandable. When you're a bit on the podgy side I suppose you won't have much luck with the ladies, so why not have a bash at the lads, eh?**

That said, you seem to do alright for a fat chap. You've had a few skinny women as girlfriends by all accounts, and it's clear your lovely wife Melanie doesn't seem to mind. Then I suppose she's got her pets to keep her company when you're out wining and dining your other ladies. I think you got her a cat, didn't you? I heard you on the TV talking about women and their pussies.

Oh, while I'm writing, can I ask about your new policy on climate change? I saw you've not thrown your American hat in the ring with this Kyoto protocol nonsense. Well done! The weather here in Llanaber is atrocious. The sooner it warms up the better, as far as we here are concerned. It costs me personally a fortune in heating bills, and apart from two weeks in July, I'm sewn into my thermals all year, and that can get a bit whiffy, believe me. Do what you can, anyway.

Thanks again and give my best to your lovely wife and your daughter, Wanka.

Best regards

David
Parish Council Foreign Secretary, Llanaber, Wales"

** OOPS! I think I made a bit of a faux pas. I remember seeing you on the news holding hands with that French chap. Well, live and let live, eh? Mind you, I don't know how you'll fit *him* in with everything else you've got on.

TEN REASONS TRUMP SHOULD GET NOBEL BUNG

I'm in Mrs. T's bad books again. She has read my letter from last week and has made criticisms. Apparently, I failed i my effort to be outward looking, i.e. push Llanaber. I've been 'encouraged' for the next effort to inform the world about events in Llanaber whilst simultaneously informing the residents of Llanaber about events in the world. What's more, mid bollocking, she used the expression 'warts and all' about events here which is somewhat confusing. I've decided to play safe and 'tell it like it is' so as to avoid another tongue lashing from the sweet shop Saddam.

Also, I've been given the toxic tap on the shoulder from Mrs. T's chubby-hubby, Leonard. I was in the middle of a urinating after the parish council meeting when he accosted me. He told me mid-stream that Mrs. T is quietly confident of getting the nod in her direction vis-a-vis the Nobel Peace Prize this time around.

Why? She's going to lose!

To make matters worse, there's the sniff of scandal here in the village in regards to the parish council election in 2016. Rumor has it the chap that owns the amusement arcade, an eastern European called Putin Lotzadosh, went round the village blackening the character of the only other candidate, Brenda Clinton, the owner of the village card shop. It transpires that bribes in the form of free goes on the Penny Falls machine in his arcade were offered to those eligible to vote.

FYI – Voting is restricted in our village to only those that either own shops or have the donkey & bouncy castle concessions on the beach.

Our village policeman, Robert Muller has been asked to look into the matter and from what I've heard all sorts of worms are crawling out of the woodwork. He is due to publish his report soon. I'm keeping my fingers crossed Mrs. T will be impeached and given the heave-ho. Then we can re-run the parish council elections on a free and fair basis, without external interference from the beast from the east.

The final fly in the ointment is that I've heard the boss of America (Donald Trump) also thinks he's going to be awarded the Nobel Prize for peace. Mrs. T will be sunk if Trump puts his hand up for the prize.

So, I'm chancing my arm that Mrs. T will get the chop; and I'm throwing my hat in with the chap from America. Here are ten good reasons why Donald Trump should be given the Nobel Prize for Peace as opposed to Mrs. T:

1. Mr. Trump was elected without any external interference in a free and fair democratic electoral system. There was no eastern European called Putin influencing the outcome.
2. Mr. Trump is working hard to warm up the planet. Mrs. T won't even turn the heating up in her shop.

3. Mr. Trump is spreading peace and harmony across one of the most troubled regions in the world, Washington. On top of that he's doing his bit in the middle east to help all those not seeing eye to eye to get along a bit better. Admittedly he's stopped chipping in to help Iran buy a bomb but he's moving his head office (America Jewish branch) from Tel Aviv to Jerusalem. That's bound to cheer up the Palestinians. As most of them are manual laborers they will benefit from the extra work knocking up a suitable block of offices for his staff.
4. Mr. Trump *never* tells lies, fact! Whereas Mrs. T tells massive porkers. She claims to sell the best fudge in Llanaber! My ass! Hers isn't a patch on the fudge sold by Mrs. Clinton in the card shop.
5. Mr. Trump publicly claims to like British shit Nigel Farage. This is a magnificent act of merciful benevolence. Farage is a slime-ball that no one else in the world can stand. (Sorry, I shouldn't have used such an offensive word, especially in an article about Mr. Trump who would never dream of calling someone a slime-ball).
6. Mr. Trump is comfortable around gays. He's just become pally with that fat lad who runs North Korea who recently 'came out.' Mrs. T can't stand them. I once told her I liked Liberace and she went ballistic. She screamed at me, 'Romans, one, twenty six to twenty seven, even their women exchanged natural sexual relations for unnatural ones. In the same way, men committed shameful acts with other men and received in themselves the due penalty for their error. Even the bible says they're bent!' I found the outburst demeaning and not worthy of the leader of the parish council. At least concede they're always well turned out.
7. Mr. Trump is orange, a much more acceptable color than Mrs. T's grey.

8. Mr. Trump has a beautiful wife, Melanie, who could be a lingerie model if she ever wanted to do a day's work. Also, Trump has a charming daughter, Wanka (likewise with the model thing). However, Mrs. T is married to chub-hub Leonard who is a lard-ass by any definition of the body mass index. He doesn't need much water in the bath, believe me! And the fruit of their loins, their three sons, Ronald, Barnie and Ernie sure as hell don't suffer from anorexia. If the whole family was rendered down there'd be enough residual tallow to build a life-sized model sperm whale candle. Further, her three boys are as dull as a nun's night life and glum faced. Whereas, whilst I've never seen Melanie smile, Wanka grins like an idiot every time there's a camera pointing in her direction. I'm surprised she hasn't suffered from paralysis of the cheeks.

9. Mr. Trump never breaks his word (Kyoto and the Joint Comprehensive Plan of Action don't count as the previous boss(es) of America signed those). Whereas, Mrs. T promised all and sundry that her 'out of code' liquorice allsorts would be sold off to parish councillors at discounted prices. Then she gave the lot to her greedy kids! I'm not a man to bear grudges but…

10. Most importantly of all, Mr. Trump wants to keep America safe. To this end he is in favor of giving everybody in the US at least one gun. His theory is that the more guns there are out on the streets, the safer citizens will be. This is especially the case for school children. He believes that if every five-year-old and older person carried a half decent shooter there would be no more violence in schools. You can't argue with that logic. Whereas Mrs. T is nowhere near as forward thinking. She won't even allow knuckledusters in the local primary school, let alone semiautomatic weapons.

So, in a plea to the Nobel Peace Prize panel, Please! Give it to Donald Trump. He *deserves* it a lot more than Mrs. T does.

That's it for now. Keep safe.

Cheerio!

AMERICA HEAD OFFICE (JEWISH BRANCH) RELOCATION UPSETS LOCALS

Photo by Bravo Prince on Unsplash

There's been big trouble in the next village along, Druidellau, and I mean BIG! What's more it's all down to Mrs. T. I'll give you the background.

Mrs. T owns a second 'Nanny Trim's Sweets 'N' Stuff' shop on the high street in Druidellau. In the parish council meeting yesterday out of the blue she suddenly announced she was moving the shop from the high street to the Arcade on the sea front. The Arcade is the prime spot in that village but nobody has ever opened a shop there. Why? Because the ownership of the site is in dispute, and has been for years.

There's a rich and powerful bunch called the Druids who run just about everything everywhere around here, and Mrs. T is as thick as thieves with them. The Druids claim to have the leasehold to the Arcade but there's a family of travelers that have been camping on the beach for years who also claim ownership. Their claim is that their great great Grandfather owned it but got 'Hamas'ed' one night and accidentally fed the only copy of the deeds to his donkey by mistake. There's been a stand-off ever since between the two sides. So, when Mrs. T upped and moved her shop lock, stock and barrel overnight there was a real dust up this morning.

I have to say it was a pretty one-sided affair. There are hundreds of travelers. They don't get any TV signal in that area so they breed like bloody rabbits. But it's not about numbers, it's about weaponry. The Druids have better fire power. The travelers only have balls of wet sand to throw, whereas the Druids have a pack of 'Devil Dogs' - a dozen half-starved Alsatians and a three legged Rottweiler. It was no contest. The dogs routed the travelers, sending them all off packing with the butts torn out of their trousers.

I'm sure we haven't heard the last of this one yet, though.

When I was thinking about the above, and what to write in the newsletter I was minded of Mr. Trump.

He recently unilaterally decided to move his American head office – Jewish branch, but his was the other way round, I think, i.e. from the coast to a village. I haven't heard anything about that move due to the perpetual fog not lifting yet so there's no TV signal in the village. But I'm sure *his* move went without a hitch. It will have been a damned site better planned than Mrs. T's debacle, I'll wager. Mr. Trump, being the boss of America, by definition must be the brainiest chap over there. He would have spotted well ahead of events if any proposed relocation would have the potential to upset the locals.

Talking of Mr. Trump, I did hear that he sent his right hand man - is it Mike Pompous or Pompeii? - to visit his counter-part in neighboring Mexico. Whilst there, Mr. P insisted on telling all and sundry the USA and Mexico are "neighbors, allies and friends." It's good to hear this kind of thing being said out loud. I know Mr. Trump banged on a lot during his election campaign about building a wall between the two countries, and I have to confess I didn't really understand the logic. So, I borrowed an atlas from the village library and looked up where the wall would be built. When I saw where it was I thought, 'Bugger me! It'd have to be huge!'

But now I see the end game. Mr. Trump, in his usual self-effacing way, is spreading peace and harmony elliptically, so as not to take the credit. He's so smart (and I think he's had that put in official records over there to make it true). Mr. Trump knows the boss of Mexico is skint. He also knows the lads that live down in Mexico of working age don't have anything to do. There isn't that much work around in their country other than making traditional Mexican artifacts to sell to tourists along with the recreational drugs. So, to help out, Mr. Trump plans to build a bloody great big pointless wall, employing the Mexicans to knock it up. Plus, there's a hidden bonus to the quaint little nation of taco munchers. When it's finished, they'll have something to kick a ball against to fill in the time.

I for one can't wait for that wall to go up. It's been a long time since Mexico performed well in the soccer World Cup. With all the extra practice their footballers will be able to put in kicking their balls against the wall, and the subsequent weight loss due to them all being broke and starving, the Mexican team should at least make the 2022 quarter finals on a shoe-in!

I understand that Mexican President Enrique Peña Nieto is cock-a-hoop about the way things are going with Mr. Trump. In the spirit of reciprocity, he has told his men to review all bilateral relations with the United States, and, when renegotiating the North American Free Trade Agreement, with the US, to ease off a little so Mr. Trump and his side at least *appear* to get a better deal.

Well done him.

That's enough for now.

Cheerio!

NIKKI HALEY SUFFERS MYSTERY ILLNESS

More trouble in the village. The parish council meeting lapsed into chaos last night after dramatic scenes. Someone turned up out of the blue demanding that the council debate the punch-up outside the Arcade in Druidellau yesterday. He was the head man from the traveling community. After some argy-bargy between him and the big cheese from the Druids, Benjy Yahoo, (who just happened to be delivering a box of free cakes to Mrs. T by way of a thank you for relocating her shop), a motion was called to debate the matter.

So, we all settled down to listen to what we expected would have been Llanaber's usual stance on any punch up between the Travelers and the

Druids, i.e. an even-handed denunciation of any violence from either side, but with a subtle bias towards the Druids, thanking them for their constraint for not turfing the Travelers off the beach completely. To everybody's horror Mrs. T immediately launched into a vitriolic polemic trashing the Travelers and slapping the Druids on the back for exercising restraint - they only kick the shit out of the men, women and male children this time, leaving the girls and babies without visible bruises.

This is just a small extract from her very long rant:

"Those Travelers are nothing short of a lazy bunch of moaning assholes! When they can't get what they want they *throw sand*, for Chrissakes!
The Druids told me one of their Devil Dogs was nearly blinded. How would *you* feel if you had a bunch of Pikeys living next door chucking sand at you every day?"

Then, when she'd finished, and just as the chap from the Travelers was about to put his point of view, to everyone's astonishment she stood up and ran out of the room!

As you can imagine, there was uproar. The chap from the Travelers was in tears.

When I got home later I switched on the TV in the hope that the perpetual fog had lifted and there would be TV signal.

There was.

The news was on. Nikki Haley, Mr. Trump's Head of Sales at the United Nations, was yelling at the Palestinians for allowing themselves to get shot. Suddenly she upped and walked out of the room, just as the heavily bandaged chap from Palestine stood up to speak. It reminded me of what Mrs. T had done earlier. I was dumbfounded. Unlike Mrs. T, Nikki Haley seems like such a nice lady who would never knowingly offend anyone, let alone the spokesperson for a group of people that have been thrown off their property then oppressed and persecuted by the very people that had stolen all their stuff.

Then I thought about what was really happening. Yes, I'd seen this behavior from women before. In our village the 'young maidens' often behave like that, suddenly standing up and rushing out of the room. There is an illness we call 'being touched by the finger of 'Titis' for which the doctor here prescribes fresh cranberry juice. I've asked the parish's head of charitable donations and overseas aid to see if there's enough funds to send Nikki Haley a crate of cranberry juice to help her along. After all, we don't want to ignite world war three just because the head of US sales can't take a proper leek.

Talking of world war three, I saw on the news that fat lad who is the boss of North Korea is threatening to throw his toys around again.

Understandably so. He's hardly just come out and made friends with Mr. Trump when his new boyfriend, that chap who runs the other half of Korea, is organizing a shooting party next door and hasn't invited him. Kim Jong Un isn't short of guns. He has loads of the things. What's more, *his* soldiers can march in neat lines and are always well turned out (if a little on the thin side). The pictures on the TV showed the lads from the south were all over the place. Not one of them looked as if he could march in a straight line while looking left. So, here's a plea from Llanaber:

Moon Jae-in, get your act together! If you want to hang on to Kim Jong Un as your new paramour, then swallow your pride and send him an invite.

It's good to see someone other than the self-effacing Mr. Trump doing their bit to help build Mexico's economy. I saw an article about the wannabe Governor of Georgia, Michael Williams. He has a campaign bus with the words, "Follow Me to Mexico" written on the back. Well done! The more American citizens you can encourage to take a mini-break to buy their recreational drugs in Mexico, the more you'll be helping the Mexicans get their shit together. There should be more forward-thinking liberals like Williams stepping up to the plate to help their neighbors along.

That's all for now.

Cheerio!

TRUMP / KIM MEETING MAY BE RELOCATED TO LLANABER

Bit of tittle-tattle first from the village. Mrs. T's chubby-hubby, Leonard, was quietly whisked into hospital yesterday. It transpires that, unbeknown to all in the village, the porcine spouse of our esteemed leader had been fitted with a gastric band. It was either that or buy a wider bath. The emergency operation carried out on him was to correct a 'mistake' in the original surgery.

The village hospital used to be world class but Mrs. T has been plundering its budget to fund amongst other things her 'fact finding' visits to the Caribbean during the winter months. In consequence, all operations are now carried out by candlelight. The story goes that the diagram for

Leonard's operation got too close to a candle and caught fire. The upshot was that the gastric band was fitted to his ass-hole, not his stomach.

Nobody suspected the error, despite Leonard putting on six stone in the three weeks after the operation. It only came to light when Mrs. T mentioned she was going to pass a motion on the village sewage system in the next council meeting, and Leonard remarked, 'I could do with passing one of those!'

Mrs. T has issued a press release saying she has visited Leonard three times already, but I know for a fact this is a lie. I heard her say, "I'm going nowhere near the fat bastard till they've cleared the backlog and mopped up the seepage."

I read that Mr. Trump's thin wife, Melanie is also in hospital. I trust they fitted her gastric band better than they did poor old Leonard's.

I read that Rex Tillerson, the rich, elderly non-politico that got the heave-ho from Mr. Trump, is giving speeches all over the US asking Americans "not to follow Trump." What a guy! Have you seen the size of *his* ass? I was surprised at the time when Mr. Trump gave this chap the big elbow, but after a remark like that, well, Mr. Trump called it right yet again.

I've heard Mr. Trump isn't exactly a healthy eater, but when you're the boss of America, you have to do a lot of lunches and posh dinners. So, being a lard-ass himself is not his fault, it goes with the territory. Can you imagine it, though? Day after day, just as you start tucking into your bucket of KFC, old Tillerson wobbles round the corner and pulls a long face. Now he's been sacked Tillerson would be better spending his time focusing his energies on something more constructive, such as warning us against politicians that repeatedly lie to the American people.

That said, it's about time a chubby, wealthy, white establishment figure in the US with no axe to grind, spoke out for improved dietary habits over there. Large, wealthy international sugary drinks companies and fast food conglomerates should lobby the US government hard to do something about it.

On the subject of Mr. Trump's weight, in all honesty, he could do with losing a few pounds, and soon, otherwise he may start to lose his boyish good looks. Apart from his delicate hands he is huge. I believe he was blimp shaped when he married Melanie. Heaven alone knows what his thin (lingerie model potential) wife ever saw in the multi-billionaire self-effacing lusty plutocrat.

Giuliani, Mr. Trump's consigliore from the Godfather, has told 'Robbie the Bobbie' Mueller that Mr. Trump can't be indicted while he's sitting. This is good news for Mr. Trump as he seems to spend a lot of time on his ass, behind desks and such. Over here the word indictment is rarely used, so I looked it up. It means formerly accused of, or charged with, a crime. I was gobsmacked. Mr. Trump *never* tells lies (fact). He said so himself! So, how on earth can he have ever have committed a crime?

After last night's parish council meeting I asked Mrs. T about what was really going on over there in the US. She's as thick as thieves with the Druids and they know everything about everything. She winked at me and whispered, 'Putin.' This made me even more confused. What the hell has the owner of an amusement arcade in Llanaber got to do with the boss of America?

The little fat lad that runs North Korea is threatening to pull out of his meeting with Mr. Trump. They were planning to have their carousal in Singapore soon. I think I know why he's done this. Dating can be awkward, especially the first one. Neither party would want to come across as too keen. As both Mr. Trump and Kim Jong Un would be traveling, neither wanted to be seen by all and sundry as the first to arrive. I have a solution.

Drop Singapore in favor of Llanaber!

Here's why:

The perpetual fog will not have lifted. It only disappears for the first two weeks of October. As a consequence, the later party would appear to have been too dumb to find the venue, and the first to arrive can then claim to be the smarter of the two. So, there is an incentive for them both to turn up together.

Mrs. T has told me to mention that the spare room at the back of her sweet shop in the village high street is available for short term hire. Tea and Turkish Delight can be provided at an extra charge (but regretfully there is no KFC in the village).

That's it for now,

Cheerio

TRUMP FAILS US KIDS – AGAIN!

Interesting developments following the horrific Santa Fe shooting in the US. At the parish council meeting last night Mrs. T stood up and gave the council another of her vitriolic polemics. This one lasted an hour and was aimed at the failings of the boss of America, Donald Trump. She was all over the place like a mad woman's doo-dahs, but in essence what she said was as follows:

The situation in the US is out of control. School massacres have become so normal people are anaesthetized to the horror. There is only one place where the buck should stop for this situation, at the White House, specifically at the door of the Oval Office.

Donald Trump has failed the American people.

Why? - Because he has yet to do a deal with the NRA to supply discounted firearms to schoolkids. As the boss of America, and, as a man that boasts (surprisingly – he's normally very self –effacing) about being a top-notch negotiator, he should have struck a deal by now. This is especially urgently needed for school children in the poorer areas. According to Mrs. T, these kids should all be given at least one hand gun each to make their schools much safer. The more senior employees (teachers, assistants, dinner ladies, security guards, caretakers, gardeners, crossing guards, secretarial staff and other administrators) should all be issued with semi-automatic weapons to up the safety level even further.

The logic is impeccable. If someone enters a school firing a gun, and there was an armed security guard crouching in the bin compound outside trying to make himself invisible, humming loudly with his fingers in his ears so he doesn't hear the screaming, these atrocities could never happen.

Apparently, the perpetual fog lifted last night and Mrs. T got TV signal and saw the story of the school shooting on the news. She was moved to tears.

"Nothing like the events that happened in Santa Fe school will ever happen in Llanaber," she ranted, "To this end, to keep our children safe and with immediate effect, every child from five years old upwards will be issued with free a ball-peen hammer and a set of knuckledusters.

FYI – She's not a cheapskate over the costs for shooters, it's just that unless you're a Druid or one of their clique, guns are hard to come by in Llanaber.

When her proposal was put to the council, I for one voted for the motion to be carried. It went through unopposed. Funds plundered from the village hospital budget will be released tomorrow and I've been given the job of securing supply. I can get a really good deal on second hand knuckledusters from a pal I have in the Traveling community but I think that would be a bad move. If the Druids found out I was trading with them I'd be blackballed.

I have another chum that can get cheap hammers from Iran. I'll give him a try.

Afterthought – I saw Mr. Trump on TV bemoaning the tragedy. He said, "These shootings have been going on too long."

What a hypocrite! America is a rich nation. If he upped the budget and got his finger out, he could supply all the kids with semi-automatics. That way the shootings would be over much quicker.

I saw Giuliani (Mr. Trump's consigliore from the Godfather) on the TV last night. I must say, he looked pretty rattled to me. He was being asked what the difference was between Clinton (who Giuliani said *could* be indicted when sitting) and Trump (who Giuliani said *could NOT* be indicted when sitting). The plump bit player from the Godfather started wringing his hands, moaning and shouting at the interviewer that this wasn't fair. The two situations are entirely different.

Why? If you're sitting down, you're sitting down, surely?

The chap that looks after the overseas aid budget here in Llanaber gave me the nod last night that a crate of cranberry juice has been dispatched to the UN, addressed to Nikki Haley, Head of Sales (America). Hopefully if she downs a few pints of the stuff she won't embarrass herself by having to suddenly up and run out of UN Security meetings again. 'Titis' is the woman's curse, even more so than visits from 'Aunt Irma.'

Just to fill you in on what's happening here. Prince Harry (the ginger guy with the beard from the royals) is getting married today to Angela Merkel. I must confess it surprised me when they announced their engagement. She seems quite sensible, and he's a lot younger than her. I suppose, being a royal, it was a 'duty' thing to re-establish our royal family's links to the Germans, what with Brexit about to happen here. The royals (B team) tried to do a lot of that during the war, so historians tell us, because the Germans looked like winning at the time. But the boss of the Germans, Adolf Hitler, gave them the bum's rush. He already had enough freeloaders to deal with and a bloody war to lose.

That's it for now.

Cheerio!

TRUMP SAVE THE US GAZILLIONS YET AGAIN!

There's a whiff of scandal in the parish. Apparently the head of the parish council, Mrs. Trim, is having an extension built on her luxury mansion.

So what? (I hear you say).

It just happens to be exactly the same size and shape as the village's planned (but never built) new leisure center. It has an Olympic sized pool, squash court, tennis court, fitness room, changing rooms, sauna, steam room, hot tub and an ice skating rink. True, Mrs. T is worth a few bob. Her sweet shop in the high street has a reasonable turnover. But she's nowhere near rich enough to afford a building like the one she's putting up. The local cop (Robbie the Bobbie) was asked to take a look into the matter.

However, just as the taxi turned up to take him and his family on their six week fact finding trip to Bermuda financed by the council (from plundered hospital funds) and signed off by Mrs. T, he said he doesn't do white collar criminal investigations.

He added, "Mrs. T would never dream of syphoning off the council dosh from the leisure center project into her own bank account then brazenly build the bloody thing as a garage extension. It's something I specifically told her not to do. No one in the village is above the law in Llanaber, y'know!"

Nevertheless, questions were asked in the council chambers. Mrs. T was asked to explain where the ring fenced funds for the leisure center had disappeared to.

"I'd show you where every penny was spent," she screeched at her accusers, "had the only copy of the project accounts not been, regrettably, burned and totally destroyed in a tragic filing cabinet fire in my office yesterday."

She added, "The new leisure facilities are in hand, on schedule and will be delivered within budget and on time."

By this she's referring to the two swings and a see-saw that have just been put up behind the bus stop in the high street.

Very poor!

On further questioning, Mrs. T added, "The original plan put forward would have cost the council a £billion, billion, billion. I made a few economies, and, because of all the work I put into this, I feel justifiably entitled to pocket a percentage of the money saved.

It'll probably turn out to be 100% of the money ring-fenced for the leisure center.

I wish we had a leader like Donald Trump rather than her. The self-effacing orange faced boss of America has just worked a miracle with their building funds budget. Apparently one of his lads tried to pull a fast one regarding the budget for their new office (America – Jewish branch). The Dumbo tried to get the budget for the new Jerusalem branch signed off by Mr. Trump by disguising it as a belated 'best wishes' leaving card for their top-cop, James Comey (recently sacked for deliberately doing his job). The minion told Mr. Trump that everyone else in the office except the President had signed the card. But Mr. Trump wasn't fooled. He saw through the silly ploy and looked at the bunch of papers underneath where he was asked to sign.

He hit the roof.

The bill for the America – Jewish branch building was going to be a $billion, billion, billion! He took out his red pen and, in a matter of minutes, had whittled the bill down to $67. He did it with his left hand while his right hand was writing out a new set of facts for his consigliore from the Godfather, Rudy Giuliani, regarding 'other matters.' What a man!

Let's hope this rotund, Fanta colored, self-effacing, fanny magnet of a man doesn't do like our Mrs. T did and pocket the savings.

It's good to see Mr. Trump's thin, lingerie model potential wife, Melanie, back home after her gastric band operation, although I heard Mr. Trump got into hot water by calling her Melania by mistake in a tweet.

Fair play to him, though. Even after taking into consideration his tiny hands, his thumbs are a bit on the podgy side. It can't be easy to hit the keypad on an iPhone with those sausage sized suckers.

The perpetual fog lifted last night and I managed to catch an item about Jimmy Carter giving an inaugural address at Liberty University. The old duffer was burbling on something about *his* being bigger than Mr. Trumps.

So what?

We are what God made us. Yours may be bigger than Donald Trump's, Mr. Carter, but he's had a lot more girlfriends than you, despite the reputed size difference.

I understand there's a statue of Mr. Trump 'in the nude' going up for auction in Jersey City. Perhaps this piece of art will finally dispel rumors about the size of Mr. Trump's 'hands.' I presume Mr. Trump posed naked for the sculptor. I'm sure Mr. Trump, being good with figures, would have ensured the proportions were neither exaggerated nor... the other one (inaggerated?).

To be honest, I thought Ex-President Carter died years ago, but that's the problem with living in Llanaber. Due to the perpetual fog, it's hard to keep up to date with who's kicked the bucket and who hasn't.

That's it for now.

Cheerio.

IRANIAN HIT SQUADS – LLANABER AT RISK

President Donald Trump poses for photos with ceremonial swordsmen on his arrival to Murabba Palace, as the guest of King Salman bin Abdulaziz Al Saud of Saudi Arabia, Saturday evening, May 20, 2017, in Riyadh, Saudi Arabia. (Official White House Photo by Shealah Craighead)

Big news in the village. Mrs. T, the head of the village parish council, has gone into hiding. She hasn't been seen anywhere in the village since she heard the 'boss of war' in America, Mike Pompeii, start telling everyone the Iranian revolutionary guard are (or is it is?) carrying out assassinations in the heart of Europe.

Mrs. T, in her befuddled mind, thinks Llanaber is the true geographical center of the European Community territories. I don't know why she thinks this. I once borrowed the village globe from the library and looked at precisely where we were relative to places like Brussels, Paris, Madrid,

Rome, and Berlin, and to be honest, we're nowhere near the middle.

But why has Mr. Pompeii's bizarre assertion frightened Mrs. T? (I hear you say).

Well, you may recall that she got herself into a flat spin when the boss of America, Donald Trump, threatened to impose sanctions on anyone trading with Iran. She buys, or to be more precise *bought*, her Turkish Delight from a supplier that she thought may have been getting the stuff from Iran, but was, in fact, quite properly getting supplies from North Korea. She sensibly ditched that supplier and to play safe now buys all the sweets for her shop through the guy that runs the amusement arcade, the 'beast from the east' Putin Lotzadosh.

You may also recall that following the horrific Santa Fe school shootings, Mrs. T put a campaign in motion to make the village school safer for kids. This she started after seeing the dreadful hash Donald Trump is making of things in America by not supplying hand guns to all the over fives, and semi-automatics to all school staff over there. Determined to be ahead of the curve, she told me to get off my butt and organize supplies of knuckledusters and ball-peen hammers for the kids in the village.

I was only following orders (where have I heard that before?).

I bought six hundred hammers off a pal I know in Iran. His were half the price of the ones on sale in the village hardware shop so I thought I'd scored a goal. Even Mrs. T agreed at the time.

"The boy's done well," I heard her whisper to her blubby-hubby, Leonard. Her pen was hovering over the document that diverted funds from the village hospital into a fact-finding trip to Sea World Orlando for me and my family to study human / fish interaction techniques for the local chip shop. She would have signed off the trip had I not stupidly told her where I was getting the hammers from.

She went apoplectic!

"You complete cretin!" she yelled at me, "I don't want that orange faced, self-effacing lard barrel (Trump?) slapping sanctions on anyone in the village, let alone me!"

It's lucky I didn't mention that I'd bought six hundred knuckledusters off the Travelers from the next village along. She's well in with the Druids who run that village (and everything else!). They'd come down on me like a ton of bricks if they found out I'd given any business to the oppressed, halfstarved Gyppos they keep hemmed in on the beach.

Any road up, Mrs. T tore up the document authorizing my trip to Orlando, then threw a box of Turkish Delight at my head.

Then she tore up the purchase order for the hammers.

Et voila!

That's why she's gone into hiding.

The loss of sales of six hundred hammers at £2 each will make a big dent in the failing Iranian economy. After Pompeii's warning, Mrs. T figured she must surely be number one on the Iranian revolutionary guard's hit list.

Mrs.T, through an intermediary (her lardy husband) has issued instructions to the village policeman (Robbie the Bobbie) to arrest anyone in the village walking about with dark skin, a turban, and a beard. The idiot is taking the instruction seriously but also literally. He is going round the village grabbing anyone with *either* dark skin *or* a turban *or* a beard and throwing them into prison. There are very few (zero) people around here that wear turbans, but there are a few with beards.

As for the dark skin, the perpetual fog lifted for a few days last week and everyone in the village has been basking in the glorious sunshine. Robbie the Bobbie is not a well-educated man, a necessary qualification for the job. He doesn't know the difference between a sun tan (a very temporary skin tonal change around here) and ethnic coloring. Consequently he's locked up all the men in the village except those who are members of the parish council. Worse, only Mrs. T can sign off the release of anyone in the cells, and she's in hiding.

We're all praying for either Mrs. T or the perpetual fog to return.

A quick word about the village infrastructure. Mrs. T took a leaf out of Donald Trump's campaign to become the big cheese. Like Trump, she promised that if elected she would improve the state of the roads in the village. We lost another four sheep this week down the sewer on the main street.

Once elected, Mrs. T gave the task of improving the roads to her brother-in-law, Elsie. (It's his nick name. His real name is Leonard Cohen Pender – his Dad was a big Cohen fan) So, to avoid confusion with her husband, Mrs. T calls him by his initials, L.C.

Elsie is known locally as 'Pender the Fender Bender Mender,' as he is the owner of the only garage in the village. Since he was given the job of improving the roads they mysteriously seem to have gotten a lot worse. When I tackled Elsie about it, he barked, "Tell me about it! My garage is working flat out around the clock seven days a week fixing the cars."

Funnily and inexplicably, one post that has never been created in either Donald Trump's cabinet or on the village council is 'Anti-Corruption and Nepotism Tsar;' wonder why not?

Mrs. T may be as bent as a corkscrew but Mr. 'Never-Told-A-Lie-In-His-Life' Donald Trump, at least, has a bunch of people around him that would be perfect for the job, Jared Kushner, Donald Trump Jr., and his wafer thin daughter, Wanka, to name but three.

That's it for now.

Cheerio!

OUTRAGE IN LLANABER AT COHEN $400K PAY OFF

Mrs. Trim, the head of the parish council here in Llanaber, is spitting blood about the news of Michael Cohen allegedly taking $400,000 to fix talks between the Ukrainian president and the boss of America, Donald Trump. When she heard the news she summoned her own lawyer to her secret hideout above her shop in the village high street. She still believes she is at the top of the Iranian revolutionary guard's hit list for cancelling the order with Iran for 600 hammers, so officially remains in hiding.

However, this is the tourist high season in Llanaber, and she can't be in hiding *and* run her sweet shop. So, her strategy is to hide from the Iranian hit squad *in clear sight*. She's as dumb as a brick (where have I heard that phrase before?).

Mrs. T's lawyer is a Druid (no shame in that) called Solly Weinstein. There's an expression in the village, 'If you want to find a golf course follow a Druid.' They spend a lot of time playing golf. Actually, this isn't fair. True, the Druids spend a lot of time on the golf course, but this is because they're trying to retrieve their lost balls. It's not easy to find them, what with the perpetual fog, and the Druids are a cost-conscious tribe.

What I'm clumsily getting round to is that I was sent to the golf club to find Solly. Mrs. T gave me a loud hailer and a tin can full of golf balls to rattle, and then sent me out onto the foggy fairways to retrieve the Druish legal-eagle.

It took an hour. I found him hiding in a bunker trying to bury himself.

"I know precisely why she wants to see me," Solly told me while surreptitiously nicking the golf balls from my tin can, "She's heard about Cohen's $400k bung."

He went on to confess that a few months ago Mrs. T had stiff armed him into back channeling a secret meeting between her and the Travelers that have been kept corralled on the beach by the Druids in the next village along. Solly had refused at first, mistakenly thinking back-channeling was a sexual preference.

"We Druids are a religious people and don't do that sort of thing," he told her.

When she pointed out it meant arranging secret talks he was up for it, especially if he could extract a fee from the oppressed, half staved and bankrupt travelers for the privilege. After lengthy negotiations the Travelers agreed to pay Solly the princely sum of £30 along with giving him access to any amount of free sand, should he ever need to concrete his drive.

Mrs. T was extremely pleased with the deal *at the time*. She kept £25 and Solly retained the residuals.

The meeting, which lasted only four minutes, duly went ahead. The Travelers pleaded with Mrs. T for food and freedom, and she promised to do everything she could to help them.

It was an empty promise, of course. Mrs. T is as thick as thieves with the Druids and wouldn't do anything to go against them. The Druids hate the Travelers. They use their 'devil dogs' to keep all the Travelers crammed onto one small sand dune on the beach.

So, with the knowledge that the boss of America's private lawyer was given a bung of $400,000 for arranging a four-minute pointless meeting with the big cheese, Solly looked as if he had under-sold his secret worthless conflab between the Travelers and Mrs. T.

"She'll want to chew my balls off," Solly told me, burying himself under the sand in the bunker.

I felt sorry for him so I lied to Mrs. T and told her he was off making another of his amateur videos with the girls in the village.

Everyone in the village was glued to their TV sets last night. The weather forecast was set for a brief spell of perpetual fog lifting, and everyone wanted to see the Steve Bannon interview on the box. The shy, modest, reclusive Bannon rarely gives an interview, and the man is a living God in our village. You can imagine the excitement when we heard he would actually be speaking on camera for once. This is the man that single handedly opened the eyes of the American people to the true genius of the cheese-ball colored, self-effacing, sexy wizard that is Donald Trump.

We all watched agog as words of unmitigated wisdom dripped from
Bannon's stubbly chin like acidic syrup off a stack of anemic pancakes with a 70's mullet hair-do. Like Trump, Bannon never lies. So when he said he *wasn't* thrown out on his ass for dissing Trump's family and friends, I for one believe him.

The ex-White House self-deprecating living legend went on to reassure the British people that, post Brexit, they could depend on Trump to keep his word and strike a deal with the UK over trade. That's very comforting to know when we're about to burn our bridges with our biggest trading partner next door.

I'm sure we won't be shunned by all the Commonwealth countries that we crapped all over when we ditched them to join the EU, and that we *can* do a deal with India without accepting mass immigration from that country.

But if things *do* go belly up with those nations, it's good to know we can rely on good ol' honest Don, a man that *always* keeps his word (… like I've said before, you can't count the 1992 United Nations Framework Convention on Climate Change, and the Iranian Joint Comprehensive Plan of Action, etc.
etc.)

That's it for now. Keep smiling.
Cheerio!

TRUMP / KIM MEETING – THE TRUTH

Source: https://www.socialnews.xyz/2017/09/22/trump-kim-re-like-children-in-a-kindergarten-russia/

The news that the boss of America, Donald Trump has called off his meeting with Kim Jong Un was a blow to Mrs. T. She had reserved the room above her sweet shop in the high street especially for this occasion. But her disappointment quickly turned to incandescent rage when she saw a copy of the letter Trump released for public consumption, the open letter sent to Kim.

She dragged me into her office and showed me a copy of the letter she was sent along with the cancellation note for the room above her shop. Upon reading the two letters side by side, I had to admit there were subtle differences. Mrs. T has demanded that I put the true version into the public domain. This I do now, reluctantly, as I believe this does not show Mr. Trump in a good light. I have always believed him to be a man above reproach when it comes to probity, honesty and self-deprecation, but I print the original obtained from

Mrs. T in its entirety, and leave you to make up your own mind. Here goes:

His excellency Kim Jong Un
Chairman of the State Affairs
Commission of the Democratic
People's Republic of Korea
Pyongyang

Dear Mr. Chinaman:
We greatly appreciate your time, patience, and effort with respect to our recent negotiations and discussions relative to a summit long sought by both parties, which was scheduled to take place on June 12 in Llanaber.

We were informed that the meeting room above Nanny Trim's Sweets 'N' Stuff shop was requested by North Korea as the venue, but that to us is totally irrelevant as you will be paying for it wherever. It could be on the polar ice cap as far as I'm concerned. That said, you chose well, little one, as Llanaber is beautiful this time of year if the fog lifts.

I was very much looking forward to being there with you and touching knees under the table. I've heard Mrs. Trim's Turkish Delight is to die for and her Fudge is the best in the village (N.B. For even handedness on behalf of the US government it should be put on record that this is a point contested by Mrs. Clinton, the lady that owns the card shop. Whilst this cannot be independently verified, she claims to put more butter in her recipe).

Sadly, based on the tremendous anger and open hostility displayed in your most recent statement about John Bolton being a loud mouthed fart, Mike Pence being an Albino lizard, and not being given permission by Mrs. Trim to have the run of the sweet shop downstairs after the meeting for free, I feel it is inappropriate, at this time, to have this hastily scheduled meeting.

Therefore, please let this letter serve to represent that the Llanaber summit, for the good of both parties, but to the detriment of Mrs. Trim, will not take place, and the bill for the £25 deposit paid to reserve the room above the shop will be winging its way to you.

You talk about your big 'hands,' but mine are so massive and powerful that I pray to God they will never have to be used for making the holes in donuts.

I felt a wonderful dialogue was building up between you, funny little rocket man, and me, to use your words, a mentally deranged U.S. dotard, and ultimately, it is only that I beat the crap out of you and your shithole of a country that matters.

Someday, I look very much forward to meeting you at Mrs. Trim's shop. In the meantime, I want to thank you for the release of the hostages you illegally imprisoned and treated like crap, but who are now home with their families giving your picture the finger. That is a beautiful gesture and here's one from me to go with theirs.

If you actually have a mind, and are capable of changing it, please think twice about ringing me. You've already made me look a chump because my shit-for-brains underlings couldn't keep their big mouths shut, so I could do without further humiliation from you, bowling ball head.

The world, North Korea, and Mrs. Trim in particular, have lost a great opportunity for lasting peace and a fat profit to Mrs. Trim for providing us with great tea. This missed opportunity is a truly sad moment for Mrs. Trim as she'd already banked the £25 and was expecting a much bigger payday for hosting a couple of gluttons like us.

Sincerely yours,

Donald J. Trump
Boss of the United States of America

With a saddened heart I sign off until next
time, Cheerio!

WEINSTEIN TURNS HIMSELF IN

It's simply amazing how often life imitates fiction. I was watching the publicity trailers for Harvey Weinstein's latest sexy rom-com romp from his franchise about male sexual harassers, (I think it's called, 'Me Too' - a film in which I see he has taken a walk on part), when it was announced in the village that Mrs. T's personal lawyer, *Solly* Weinstein (no relation) has been arrested.

Solly has had his metaphorical collar felt by the village cop, Robert 'Robbie the Bobbie' Muller while he was in the middle of filming one of his homemade videos with the girls from the village.

It was a film on Solly's usual subject, a documentary about health care. Solly, with the help of all the young maidens from the village, has made twenty eight of these videos to date. I for one have watched them all. Not only are they very competently made for an amateur, but they're also informative and entertaining. They're also very good value at £20 per 24 hours rental.

The series is called simply, 'Skincare for Girls.'

The girls are all asked to undress and lie on the beach in the fog for ten hours, during which time Solly videos their bodies in minute and sometimes intimate detail. Close-ups and unusual photographic angles are a feature of which Solly is justifiably proud. The objective is to compare from day to day whether fog bathing can cause premature wrinkling of the skin around the sensitive areas of a young lady's anatomy. Solly sincerely believes that by the time he's reached retirement age in twenty years from now, or he has prematurely gone blind, he will have the definitive answer as to this vexing question.

This is important medical research work for our community and is all carried out using money legitimately syphoned off by Mrs. T from the village hospital's budget.

Not one of the girls has ever complained – up till now.

It transpires that Solly has recently taken to insisting that each of the girls sees him alone in his private quarters before the young lady is given a part. Once he has them in his clutches he bullies them into letting him measure their belly-buttons.

When Solly cornered Brenda, the chubby lass that runs the bakery, she would have none of it. She spurned his advances and ran screaming to the police. I suspect this is because she has difficulty enough finding her own tummy canyon. So, the idea that Solly might blab all over the village about her deficiency in that area must have been too much for the poor girl, so she 'did him in.'

Solly was subsequently told by the village policeman to hand himself in at the local cop-shop by 5pm yesterday. This he did and, upon presenting himself, he was duly arrested and thrown into prison. It's pretty cramped in there these days. You may recall that Robbie the Bobbie, on Mrs. T's instructions, started arresting anyone with dark skin, *or* a turban, *or* a beard, in case they're Iranian revolutionary guard hit-men out to get her for cancelling an order with Iran for 600 hammers at £2 each.

In fact, in a moment of idiocy (a pre-requisite for the job as village cop) Robbie, after spending all day on the beach arresting people, noticed he'd developed a nice tan, so arrested himself.

Anyway, back to Solly.

Talk about the flood gates opening! Just about every other young maiden whose had a part in one of Solly's films has subsequently come forward blubbing and bleating on that they were 'abused' by the amateur video enthusiast.

How? It was medical research, for Chrissakes!

Further, Solly gave each and every one of them a £50 bung before any filming took place and a cut of the profits from the rentals. Also, he promised them all a lucrative part in his next medical research documentary series, 'Breast Sagging - The Risks Associated with Exposure to Fog.'

Hypocrites! These girls were all happy to take the money then. Why should they cry foul on him now?

Also, each and every one of them signed a non-disclosure agreement requiring them to pay back the £50 bung and any accrued royalties for the video rentals if they blabbed.

Not a single one of them has!

The obvious conclusion is that these young girls are now crapping all over Solly, not for reasons of morality, but for monetary gain. It hasn't gone unnoticed that these girls are all being offered lucrative bungs from the village newsletter for their kiss and tell stories.

No doubt when Mrs. T comes out of hiding she'll sort out the mess. She's very good at pardoning people she likes. I think she picked that trick up from George W Bush.

STOP PRESS - It's just come through on the village ticker-tape that the boss of America, Donald Trump, has issued a pardon to Sylvester Stallone for his part in the appalling Rockie movies. Well done Donald! It wasn't Stallone's fault the scripts were so bad that a superlative classical actor like him had to incoherently mumble his way through the dreadful vomit-making corn-ball dialogue in those films.

That's it for now.

Cheerio!

WEINSTEIN OUT ON BAIL – LOCK UP YOUR DAUGHTERS

How the mighty have fallen. I watched the lop-sided faced Harvey Weinstein (forceps birth injury?) perp walked into and out of the cop-shop on TV yesterday. This was followed by all the women he'd made wealthy and famous crowing about his downfall (butt-lickers turned butt-kickers).

I must confess to feeling a bit sorry for the guy. It will have been a crippling blow to the modest chap's already fragile self-esteem to discover these demure and retiring ladies were just using him.

Women eh!

It's okay for old Harv now, but what'll he do for 'comfort' when his power base has gone and he loses his good looks?

In the TV piece it was mentioned that old Harv had been discreetly electronically tagged. This modern method of controlling the movements of offenders released from prison is yet to reach Llanaber, which brings me to my point.

Solly Weinstein (no relation) was released from the village clink yesterday. He was bailed out by Mrs. T, who has decided to come out of hiding. She had read in the press that the stories about Iranian revolutionary guard hit squads operating in Europe all emanated from the same source, the boss of war for America, 'Potty' Pompeii.

Mrs. T loathes the man with a passion and doesn't believe a word that slides from his lying blubbery mouth - her words not mine. He seems like a well-rounded individual to me.

But why is Mrs. T so vitriolic about the American boss of war (I hear you say)?

The Trump / Kim meeting, of course.

Mrs. T had reserved the room above her sweet shop in the high street for their upcoming summit carousal, only to be bounced when the two high density leaders started spitting at each other, the prelude to calling the whole thing off. In fairness to Mr. Trump, it was his cretinous losers, Bolton and Pence that did the spitting on his behalf.

To make matters worse, Mrs. T had already baked and iced a batch of her famous, airy-fairy cakes. These usually sell in her shop for £2 each. She baked five hundred of the buggers, figuring the two fat-mountains would wire into the lot in a frenzied gluttonous battle to the last crumb. The one who hoovered up the most cakes could claim supremacy of the stomach.

Mrs. T would have made a small fortune. Instead she will probably lose money on the event, especially if she has to ditch the cakes. Mrs. T's airyfairy cakes have a shelf life of eighteen days in normal ambient conditions and only twelve when the perpetual fog descends.

In my book she was a bloody fool for getting ahead of herself. The meeting wasn't scheduled till June 12th, so she was taking a gamble making them so soon. I know there are rumblings in the media that the meeting could still take place but Mrs. T is risk averse. She's already renting the room above the shop for that date to the Druids.

The Druids and the Travelers are in tentative peace talks. There are rumors that the Druids may make a gesture of good will towards the Travelers. They may turn back on the hose pipe to the sand dune where the Druids keep the Travelers corralled. The Druids' boss, Benjy Yahoo, is feeling a bit guilty for setting the devil dogs on them last week.

I digress. Back to Solly.

As I said, Llanaber police do not yet have the ability to discreetly electronically tag anyone released on bail. Instead the village policeman (Robbie the Bobbie Muller) chains a large pig to the subject's right leg. The logic is impeccable. It is possible that someone with an electronic tag fitted could do a runner, but you won't get far with a ten stone Welsh pig shackled to your ankle.

However, this form of 'tagging' is particularly cruel to Solly. Being Druish, he has an aversion to anything porcine. So, having one chained to your leg twenty-four seven must be hard for the amateur girlie video maker to endure.

There is also a significant health risk. In order to try and fill in the sink hole in the high street, Mrs. T has issued instructions that all village waste is to be thrown into it. This includes vegetable matter and food waste. There is a risk that should Solly go shopping in the high street, the pig sniffs the malodorous gases now emanating from the sink hole and makes a bolt for it. Poor Solly could be dragged into it by his ankle and never be seen again.

It's good to see Wanka Trump, Donald Trump's thin grinner of a daughter, taking her place on the world stage, speaking out for important global matters. Who says she's as dumb as a brick? By taking a shot at the WTA for the non-seeding of Serena Williams for the French tournament after her maternity holiday, it's clear this young lady has her finger on the pulse of what really matters to blue collar Americans and the displaced millions in the world. Let's hope that when Donald kicks the bucket, she'll be there in the background to slip seamlessly into his shoes and take the helm.

A Trump dynasty – how do you like them apples?

That's it for now.

Cheerio!

ARMING SCHOOLKIDS BACKFIRES

Mayhem in the village primary school yesterday and the blame must fall at the door of the boss of America, Donald Trump. My previously unshakeable belief in the rotund, Fanta colored self-declared Brainiac's infallibility is beginning to crumble. Several recent events have forced me to this conclusion:

The 'sod off' open letter Trump sent to Kim Jong Un, the boss of North Korea who recently 'came out.' This was clearly written on the back of a cigarette packet by a petty-minded jilted John, getting his revenge in first. Okay, there was a bit of spitting between subordinates, but for heaven's sake, grow up!

Trump's relocation of his American Head Office (Jewish branch) from Tel Aviv to Jerusalem. This move-of-madness prompted a 'me too' (no relation) reaction from the head of the village council here, Mrs. Trim. She promptly opened a second branch of her sweet shop in the Arcade on the sea front in the next village along, Druidellau. There's been nothing but trouble there between the Druids and the Travelers ever since.

Before I could have bought Ball-peen hammers to issue to the school-kids to help keep them safe for just £2 each from my pal in Iran. But after Trump's withdrawal from the Iran nuclear deal and his threat of sanctions on anyone dealing with Iran, I was forced to cancel that order by Mrs. T who went into hiding in plain sight to avoid becoming a victim of an Iranian revolutionary guard hit squad. I've now had to order them from the village hardware shop at £4 each! This means syphoning off an extra £1,200 from the village hospital budget. Dr. Mengele, who runs the hospital, has complained bitterly about the reduction in his budget. He's had to cancel the hip replacement operation on old Mrs. Winfrey, the village gossip, and cancel the 'corrective' surgery on Mrs. T's chub-hub, Leonard's gastric band. (It turns out it *was* fitted correctly when applied to his butt-hole – it works by incentivizing the wearer to reduce food consumption or risk a crap explosion).

As for Trump's idea of arming schoolkids with weapons to keep them safe, quite frankly it's a joke, which brings me to the recent mayhem in the village school.

You may be aware from my previous letters that I did a deal for 600 knuckledusters at £2 each from a Traveler friend of mine. They turned up yesterday. I personally handed out one each to the under-fives that attend the junior school in the village. I gave them strict instructions that these weapons were only to be used when they felt under threat of violence. It transpired that the school principal, Mr. Dodry, took the school morning assembly's calisthenics session, stretching and toe touching. His instruction to the children assembled in front of him was 'Do like I do, kids.'

He had the misfortune to break wind while touching his toes. The kids duly followed suit. Let's just say there were accidents. Dodry went mediaeval and started waving his arms about and yelling at the kids. Understandably they felt threatened. So they fell upon the aging educator and gave him a harsh beating with their knuckledusters.

We've had to temporarily close the school and take back the knuckledusters from the kids. Dodry is threatening legal action. At least we think he is. It's difficult to understand him as he's head to toe in plaster and his jaws are wired together.

So, my advice to you, Mr. Trump, based on our experience here, is to think again about handing out weapons to school-kids to keep them safe.

I noticed that Republican Congressman Dana Rohrabacher is getting a lot of heat in the press over in the US about his position on selling homes to 'differently ugly-bumpers (DUBs).' I for one agree with him. My next-door neighbor sold his house to a couple of DUBs last year. It's been hell living next door to them. They're so clean and always well turned out. It drives me up the wall. What's more, my 'better 70%' is always on my back with her, "Why can't you be more like them and smarten yourself up?" and "Isn't it about time *you* knitted a winter jacket for the cat?' and "Don't you *dare* tell them to turn it down! I love Judy Garland." Dana? Isn't that a girl's name?

I noticed on the village ticker tape that the trial of the boss of America's ex-campaign manager Paul Manafort has been postponed till July 24. Unfortunately, the ticker tape ran out so I didn't get the end of the message.
Which year?
That's it for now.
Cheerio!

TRUMP / KIM SUMMIT – LLANABER STILL HOPEFUL?

Is it on or is it off? This confusion i driving Mrs. T up the pipe. She is furious about the boss of America's 'will he / won't he' dithering over his carousal with the little fat lad that runs North Korea, the one that has just 'come out.'

After Trump cried off, Mrs. T provisionally accepted a booking from the Druids for the room above the shop for June 12th. Then the news broke that the summit meeting might be back on again. It said on the news (the perpetual fog lifted for an hour yesterday and we got TV signal) that minions from both sides are holding preparatory talks in Singapore ahead of a potential Trump / Kim summit there.

What is going on? Singapore was just a decoy. We understood that if the meeting took place it would be held in Llanaber, above Mrs. T's shop in the high street. As village foreign secretary responsible for international matters, Mrs. T has instructed me to write directly to Mr. Trump to get this matter cleared up once and for all. So, here goes:

"Dear Mr. President,

Re the matter of your meeting with the boss of Korea, Kim Jong Un, is this meeting actually going to take place, or is this just another PR stunt to make you look more like a rough, tough street-fightin' negotiator and less like a dithering twit?

You originally agreed to rent the room above Mrs. Trim's sweet shop from 2pm to 3pm on June 12th this year, and sent a £25 deposit. Then you cancelled and had the audacity to ask for the deposit back. This Mrs. Trim quite rightly refused to do. A deal is a deal and you are supposed to be a man of your word (Kyoto protocol, Trade agreements, the Iran nuclear deal and your marriage vows notwithstanding).

We've all seen in the news that Kim Jong Un and Moon Jaein seem to be 'hitting it off.' I can see that this must put you at a bit of a disadvantage, what with you being a 'round eye,' but that doesn't oblige you to travel to an eastern country to meet the fellow.

Come on, Mr. President, strap a pair on! You should fess up, hold the line and stick with your commitment to having this meeting in Llanaber.

Don't forget there is the issue of security to be considered. The streets in Llanaber are much safer than anywhere in Singapore now that we've taken the knuckledusters back off the five-year olds.

Also, we have entertainment organized. Assuming the perpetual fog lifts, we've planned for you both to have a 'hand-in-hand' stroll up the beach to Druidellau where the Druids have arranged synchronized beatings of the Travelers, and a display of traditional hunting of the Travelers' children with devil dogs.

Mrs. T has even organized for extra chairs to be available should you wish to bring your grinning thin daughter, or your albino sidekick, Pence. I know your beautiful thin lingerie model potential wife Melanie is not likely to come as she's still recovering from her gastric band operation.

Let's call it a date, shall we? I look forward to seeing you and your entourage on June 12th at 'Nanny Trim's Sweets 'N' Stuff' shop in the high street at 2pm.

With best wishes,

David Smith

Village Foreign Secretary

P.S. Would you please re-send the £25 deposit using a cheque addressed to Nanny Trim's Sweets 'N' Stuff, High Street, Llanaber, Wales. Please make the cheque payable to Mrs. Binky Trim."

That should do the trick.

There is some controversy in the United States about Wanka Trump, the thin grinner who acts as an adviser to her father, the boss of America, Donald Trump. It would appear she tweeted photos of herself cuddling a two year old child. She is being criticized due to her father's policy of ripping children from the arms of captured undocumented illegal immigrants and whisking the kids off to God knows where. Fifteen hundred of these kids have mysteriously gone missing.

Admittedly it's a smidge on the careless side, but if it bothers the liberal, wet, live-on-your-knees, flip-flop shufflers so much then do like Wanka did. She got off her backside and went looking for them... **_and_** she found one. Who says she's as dumb as a brick? (where have I heard that expression before?). Mind you, I can see what the fuss is about. The kid in the photos doesn't even look Mexican, so it's no wonder the missing kids are hard to find.

Republican Senator Marco Rubio's criticism of Mr. Trump's immigration policy is nothing more than political opportunism and displays his own ignorance of strategic thinking, and how this policy is meant to work. Let me easily explain it for him.

A family of undocumented illegal immigrants is caught by a border guard. The parents are separated from the kids and the parents booted back into Mexico. These people now have a genuine, non-economic incentive to sneak back into the USA, i.e. to find their missing children.

More border guards are employed to stop them = more employment of US citizens.

Eventually the bloody great pointless wall is built = more employment of Mexican citizens, as no self-respecting US citizen would waste their lives building the stupid thing. As a spin-off the skinny unemployed Taco eaters can kick a ball against the wall to increase their soccer skills and give Mexico a better chance of winning the world cup.

The missing kids in the US are absorbed into left-leaning, liberal, wealthy, do-gooder families and grow up to become US Senators & Congressmen who then vote to have the wall removed. The result is more undocumented illegals sneak into the US. They get caught… and so on ad nauseam. The logic is impeccable. Everyone's a winner!

That's it for now. Cheerio!

TRUMP'S WALL SPELLS TROUBLE FOR LLANABER

It came through on the village ticker-tape last night that the boss of America, Donald Trump has had another spat with his 'pal-down-south' the boss of Mexico, Enrique Penus Nieto. At a tea and cakes do in Nashville, Mr. Trump let it slip out that he thought it only fair that the Mexicans 'chip in a few, or whatever they can spare' towards the pointless border wall he intends to erect.

Apparently, Nieto went lip-loopy again and sent a nasty tweet about the modest philanthrope, Trump. Fortunately, I don't speak Spanish so I couldn't translate the ingratiate taco-muncher's text:

"Lo siento terriblemente, viejo amigo, pero estoy temporalmente avergonzado financieramente."

I suspect, as usual, it's something vile and insulting towards the self-deprecating, cheese-ball colored US President. What an ungrateful person Nieto is. Clearly Mr. Trump is only trying to give the man a helping hand by preventing people fleeing the violence in South American countries, and by doing so, depriving their undertakers down there of much needed work. Which brings me to news of Llanaber and Mrs. T's latest brainwave.

Mrs. T, the head of the village council, is nothing if not a theft of other people's bright ideas. She has seen what Trump is trying to achieve by building his wall and has leapt with both feet onto the back of his bandwagon.

I will elucidate. As you probably know Llanaber is located a little to the south down along the coast from Druidellau where the Druids and the Travelers live in their version of peace and harmony. What you may not know is that we have another village to our south called Spanibont. I seldom talk of this failing village. It's as rough as a bear's butt there, especially after pub chucking out time. There are a lot of rowdies that go up and down the main street pushing over old ladies, barging in the lines at the post office and making cruel jokes about ugly babies.

It's not nice having a neighbor like that and, should the perpetual fog lift and the rowdies decide to use our beach, does harm to our tourist trade. These yobbos lie about in groups in the sand dunes shouting rude things at fat ladies in swimsuits and offering the tourists recreational drugs at discount prices, well below those charged by our resident dealer, 'Iolo the Dope.'

So, Mrs. T has decided to divert more funds from the village hospital budget into building a fence. I've seen the first draft of the plan. The fence will be three feet high and will run along the border between the two parishes.

"That should keep the mouthy buggers out," she declared in the council meeting, slapping herself on the back.

Honestly, she's as dumb as a brick (where have I heard that phrase before?).

I pointed out to her that the rowdies are all big lads. They could easily climb over a fence that's only three feet tall, but she ignored my intervention and went on to make the following amazing assertion.

"What's more, the residents of Spanibont will pay for it!"

Is she mad? The poor sods in that village haven't got two enchiladas to rub together. They're on the bones of their backsides. What's more, where's their incentive? They don't want to stop the rowdies from coming to Llanaber, quite the opposite. They want to get shot of the troublemaking idiots. To be honest, unlike Mr. Trump's wall, I don't think Mrs. T has thought this through properly.

Nonetheless, she has given me the job of organizing the wood, nails and labor, but provided no funds whatsoever. It transpires that the money diverted from the village hospital budget was her fee for thinking up the idea.

I have made a tentative approach to the leader of the Spanibont rowdies, Mateo the Knife. I have arranged to meet him in the 'Abandon All Hope' pub in Spanibont high street tomorrow at twelve noon. I intend to put it to him that he and his cohorts should club together and build a fence to keep themselves out of our village. He seems like a reasonably minded chap so I'm hoping these initial talks will bear fruit.

In another massive bandwagon leap, Mrs. T has stolen yet another of Mr. Trump's great ideas. She has started accusing members of the village council of being guilty of things without offering any proof whatsoever. Mrs. T saw Mr. Trump had accused Robert Mueller and his team of meddling in the US mid-terms because they were deliberately doing their jobs. Mrs. T immediately accused Mrs. Clinton, the lady that runs the card shop in the village, of not washing her hands after she'd been to the rest room. She went on to accuse Dr. Mengele, the man in charge of the village hospital, of trying to see down her blouse.

In her defense, Mrs. T had just been wiring into a plateful of Mrs. Clinton's fudge, and had her annual medical from Dr. Mengele that morning. I think it was the combined effects of a sugar rush from the fudge and having the good doctor specifically insist that Mrs. T keep her clothes on throughout the examination. These two factors probably tipped her over the edge and caused her to momentarily step outside the boundaries of acceptable decent behavior. That or she's as mad as a box of frogs – possibly another 'me too' (no relation) stolen idea off Mr. Trump.

That's it for now.
Cheerio!

FAKE ASSASSINATION RUSE FLUSHES OUT RADICAL

  Incredible events in the village yesterday, I can't believe it's not fiction. It was the usual parish council meeting last night and we all traipsed into the council meeting room at 6 pm as normal, only to be met with the most bizarre sight. Lying on the top of the meeting room table was a coffin (lid on).

  Further, sitting in Mrs. Trim's chair was her blubby-hubby, Leonard. The epithet blubby is very appropriate in this case. He was bawling his eyes out. When I asked him what was the matter he just blew his nose on his sleeve and pointed at the coffin.

  The doors behind us suddenly banged shut and there stood the village policeman, 'Robbie the Bobbie' Muller. He had a stern look on his face as if something nasty was about to go down. He asked us all to take our seats, which we obediently did. What he said next I repeat word for word below:

"I regret to inform you all that the village council chair, Mrs. Dorothy 'Binky' Trim has been murdered. What's more we have every reason to believe she was the victim of an Iranian Revolutionary Guard hit person or persons unknown."

The village top-cop then briskly produced a three-inch square Polaroid showing Mrs. T's head with an axe sticking in the top of it. There appeared to be a lot of blood. He waved the photo in the air but before any of us could examine it more closely he shoved it back in his pocket.

"Now," he continued, looking at each of us in turn with that 'I know you're a wrong 'un' expression on his face, "Have any of you got anything to say?"

Apart from Leonard's blubbing the room fell into silence.

Suddenly Mrs. Clinton, the lady that runs the card shop and Mrs. T's rival for the village top job in 2016, stood up. Again, I quote what was said verbatim below:

"If she's a goner then can we recall her three fat kids back from their fact-finding trip to Disney Orlando at the village's expense to study the effects of motion sickness on people full of fast food? We can give the money saved back to Dr. Mengele so he can pay the village hospital's electricity bill, and rid the village of candle lit operation screw ups once and for all."

Then an astonishing thing happened. The lid of the coffin flew off and Mrs. T jumped out pointing her finger at Mrs. Clinton and repeatedly yelling, "J'accuse!"

Mrs. T seemed perfectly healthy. I have to confess to being completely flummoxed at this point in proceedings. There wasn't even a mark in her head left by the axe.

"It was all a ruse," barked Robbie the Bobbie, "The photo is a fake. We hired a rubber axe from 'Mac's Magic' joke shop in the village main street, poured some ketchup on Mrs. T's head, then took the snap." "Why?" I asked.

I knew it was a stupid thing to say as soon as the words left my lips.

"To flush her out!" snapped Mrs. T, glaring at poor old Mrs. Clinton.

Mrs. T had been watching the TV again, never a good thing. She had seen all the nonsense with Arkady Babchenco in the Ukraine and decided to pull the same stunt. She has long suspected Mrs. Clinton of having 'revolutionary ideas' such as using council money for the good of the villagers and to the detriment of Mrs. T's bank balance. Now, because of the clever theatrics concocted between herself and the village cop, she had exposed the far-left views of her erstwhile opponent.

The upshot is that Mrs. Clinton has been thrown off the council for being a rabid commie and being potentially in collusion with the Iranian hit squad out to get Mrs. T.

Mrs. T's sycophants on the council were openly chanting 'lock her up!' as Robbie the Bobbie marched her from the council chambers.

This is a sad day for democracy, the return of McCarthyism to the village. We've seen it all before from Mrs. T. She gets it into her head that the village is a hotbed of communist insurrection from time to time. She banned 'Red Nose Day' last year, thinking it was an overt display of left wing mockery of her right leaning council. Troubled times ahead, I fear.

Now, I'm sure you're on tenterhooks about the big summit meeting – Is it on or off?

I am, of course, referring to the conflab between myself and 'Mateo the Knife,' the head of the rowdies from Spanibont, that failing village next door to us down the coast.

It's off - At least for the foreseeable future.

You may recall I arranged to meet Mateo in the 'Abandon All Hope' pub in Spanibont at noon today. He's cried off. I received a hand written note this morning, delivered by a rowdy and nailed to my dog. It read as follows:

"Dear Foreign Secretary (Llanaber parish),

Thank you for inviting myself and my cohorts to construct a fence to separate Spanibont from Llanaber. If I recall correctly, the key parameters you require of us are:

- That the fence be no less than 3ft high along its entirety, that being the boundary between the two parishes.

- That it should be of a wooden and nail construction as per the diagram you sent me.

- That the fence be entirely constructed at our cost and using our labor.

- That its purpose is solely to prevent Spanibont 'rowdies' from pestering your good villagers and the said 'rowdies' selling tourists recreational drugs at discounted prices, well below those on offer from your designated pusher, 'Iolo the Dope.'

- That the fence must somehow permit the free movement of Llanaber villagers into Spanibont, should they wish to do so, and permit the free movement of sheep between both sides.

After long discussions with my cohorts and having given the matter studied consideration my answer is sod off! You must be out of your tiny mind!

Please take this as confirmation that I will not be attending our meeting scheduled for 12 noon today. Up yours, and have a nice day,

Mateo the Knife.
Boss of the rowdies,
Spanibot, Wales

Quite frankly this doesn't come as a surprise, although his response is a lot more articulate and polite than I expected from the boss of the rowdies. It's nothing like the incoherent vile garbage texted by the boss of the Mexicans, Enrique Penus Nieto, when he rejected Mr. Trump's kind offer to let them pay for his wall.

That's it for now.

Cheerio!

TRUMP PARDON SCANDAL – SOLLY GETS OFF

Donald Trump, the amber colored self-effacing boss of America, is handing out pardons like candy over there. I saw in the press he's pardoned Lewis 'Scooter' Libby for his appalling acting in the film 'Fair Game' and Sylvester Stallone for his bad acting in the Rocky franchise. But it's not just actors. There was also Sheriff Arpaio, wrongly vilified just for being over-fond of racing Mexicans with his police cars.

Now Trump's considering clemency for Martha Stewart and former Gov. Rod Blagojevich of Illinois. Quite rightly too! Stewart was just unlucky selling those shares moments before the company crashed, and when questioned under oath about the matter, let's just say her memory isn't what it was. Has the judiciary over there never heard the word coincidence?

As for Blagojevich, plenty of people sell seats. What's wrong with that? There's even a furniture shop in our village that sells them for Chrissakes!

The point I'm coming round to a bit slowly is that Mrs. T has once again followed the path of righteousness blazed by Mr. Trump. She has pardoned Solly Weinstein (no relation) and ordered the village cop (Robbie the Bobbie) to unshackle the pig from his leg. You may recall that I mentioned electronic tagging hasn't reached our village yet. This he has done, but you would not believe the outcry! The village maidens are up in arms about it. They are accusing Mrs. T of cronyism for releasing the home movie pervert just because Solly is her private lawyer, which is, of course, unfair. Mrs. T has pardoned other villagers on a non-partisan basis, including Robbie the Bobbie himself. You may also recall recently, in his hunt for Iranian Revolutionary guard hit men in the village, he accidentally arrested himself for having a suntan.

Let's see if Mrs. T's mood for clemency extends to old Mrs. Clinton who runs the card shop. Yesterday she was 'exposed' in a fake assassination sting and arrested for being a leftie, pinko, live-on-your-knees, antiestablishment, revolutionary commie subversive. Her case comes up for trial next week.

It's good to hear that the thin, lingerie model potential wife of Donald Trump, Melanie, is once again firing on all one cylinder after her gastric band operation. The strength has at last returned to her tweeting thumb and she is telling the world all is well with regards to her health and her marriage. She has once again returned to her duties of eating tissue paper and not buckling under the massive burden of Mr. Trump's porcine bulk, should he have one of his frisky hot flushes. Well done Mel. Good to have you back on your feet, or whatever.

Let's talk trade sanctions and protectionism for a moment. It came through on the village ticker tape that Donald Trump has unilaterally imposed a twenty-five percent tariff on steel and aluminum imported into the US.

Llanaber has no steel or aluminum exports so you'd think this bright idea of Mr. Trump's would have no effect on the village whatsoever.

Wrong!

Not long after Trump's declaration, it came through on the ticker tape that European Commission president Jean-Claude Juncker struck back, threatening to impose tariffs on US products including Florida orange juice and Bourbon. I've said it before and I'll say it again. Mrs. T is as dumb as a brick (where have I heard that phrase before?). I know she never reads this newsletter, so I think I'm safe to express my opinion freely, after all, we live in a democracy. She thinks she's some kind of whiz kid and plans to make money out of the situation.

Here's how her massive intellect works.

She has diverted funds from the village hospital and ordered a container load of Kentucky Bourbon from the States. It arrives in three weeks. She intends to hold onto the stuff in the hope that the price per bottle will rocket once Juncker's tariffs start to bite over here. She knows the Druids are fond of a drop and are a cost-conscious tribe. Her plan is to offload the lot to them at a price marginally below market and make a killing.

Why is she dumb (I hear you ask)?

The Druids are no slouches when it comes to exploiting shifts in the marketplace. They'll be several jumps ahead of Mrs. T. and the village is bound to get burnt on the deal.

At least it's bourbon, something of use. I had to fight really hard to convince Mrs. T not to buy a container load of steel girders from the EU. She had the brainwave that the rowdies from Spanibont would jump at the chance of buying at their own expense discounted girders off her to build the fence she wants putting up to separate Llanaber from their village. If they won't cough up for a wooden fence why would they do so for steel girders? What's more Mrs. T's specification requires the fence to be constructed using nails, not easy to bash through steel joists.

Another strange happening in the village worth a mention, it was on the news that Poland has offered Donald Trump space in their country for a huge permanent US military base. Not long after this announcement, the chap that owns the amusement arcade in the village, the beast from the east, Putin Lotzadosh, made an approach to the parish council. He is offering a substantial amount of cash to the village to buy a plot of land adjacent to the estuary.

"I have some life-sized models of military equipment, boats, submarines, missiles and suchlike, I want to keep there," he told the assembled parish councilors. Then, winking at Mrs. T, he added, I"ll make it worth your while Binky, my little Babushka!" Little?

Mrs. T?

What on earth is going on?

That's it for now. Cheerio!

TRUMP/KIM – IT'S ON AGAIN! -
LLANABER PLANS CAKES

I read on the village ticker tape that Donald Trump, the orange-faced blonde comb over who is the boss of America, is putting pressure on his Energy Secretary, Rick Perry, to in turn put pressure on the energy companies in the US to keep their shagged out coal fueled power plants running, even though they belch out millions of tons of carbon dioxide into the atmosphere and are uneconomical.

Well done! Mr. Trump. It's great news for Llanaber.

Thanks to your tireless efforts to warm up the plane, the perpetual fog that is the blight of our village lifted for two days last week. That big orange thing in the sky we caught a glimpse of for those two days reminded to us of your rotund, fat, benevolent face smiling down warmly upon the village.

It's ON again! Hooray!

There was much jubilation and celebration in the council chambers last night when word came through that Donald Trump and his new paramour who has recently come out, Kim Jong Un, are to have their carousal after all. Word in the media is that the meeting will take place on June 12 in Singapore. The head of the village parish council here, Mrs. Trim, doesn't believe that for a moment. She is confident this is a masterly stroke of deception to throw the rat-pack media off the scent, so the two can have their conflab without the prying eyes of the press gaping at them, in case there's more spitting. She is convinced the meeting WILL take place in… guess where? Yes, the room above her shop right here in Llanaber.

To this end, and without yet having received a reservation booking plus the £25 deposit from the US government for the room, she has unilaterally cancelled the booking she took from the Druids. You may recall that Mrs. T, in a fit of pique when Trump cancelled last time, rented the room on that date from 2pm for an hour to the Druids. Mrs. T rarely does anything to upset this powerful tribe, so she must be confident of getting in on the act with the Trump / Kim get-together. Even as I write, I can hear the clattering sound of baking tins being greased as Mrs. T gets another batch of her airy-fairy cakes underway for the two world brainiac and anorexia deniers to wire into when she serves their tea.

Mrs. T saw in the news that Trump has just appointed Coast Guard Rear Adm. Doug Fears to be his new homeland security adviser. (If he's from the coast guard, surely he should be the home-sea security adviser!). Ever the copycat of any half decent idea she thinks Donald Trump's had, she has, without any council debate or the following of correct recruitment procedures, gone off and appointed a new head of village security.

It's a very controversial appointment, and I mean VERY controversial.

The job hasn't been given to somebody from the village as is traditional. Instead, the position has been given to none other than 'Mateo the Knife,' the boss of the rowdies from that failing neighboring village of ours, Spanibont.

What's more I can see trouble ahead. There is no love lost between the village cop and the new head of security. Our local cop, Robert (Robbie the Bobbie) Muller, has made a career out of arresting Spanibont rowdies and throwing them out of the village. The enmity between Robbie and Mateo goes right back to their schooldays when they were rivals for the hand of Mrs. T. Back then she was plain 'Binky' Butterworth, and an ornament to society – not the huge blob of tallow she is now. As it happened, in the end they both lost out to the elusive charms of the vicar's son, Leonard Trim.

It's heartwarming to see the boss of America, Donald Trump, putting world affairs to one side for a while again to tend to seemingly less important things. In this case it's to jump to the protection of his thin grinner of a daughter, Wanka. Apparently, his vitriol was aimed at the comedian (or should that be comedienne?) Samantha Bee and her waspish remark that the thin grinner was a feckless (insert the rude word here). I can fully understand why matters of state such as world peace, the economy, free trade and preventing nuclear proliferation take a back seat for something important of a personal nature like this.

NOTHING is more important to a parent than protecting that parent's child from harm. (Please note this may not apply to undocumented illegal Mexican immigrants' offspring. Losing fifteen hundred of their kids would appear to be of no consequence to Mr. Trump and his administration).

That said, I think Mr. Trump should try to grow a thicker skin when it comes to the criticism of members of his family. After all, he / they chose to be in the media spotlight. If I can offer some advice, Mr. President, try to think of Wanka as an animal. It'll make it so much easier for you to cope.

That's it for now.

Cheerio!

TRUMP THREATENS 'RELATIONSHIP' WITH CHINAMAN KIM

It came through on the village ticker tape (much more reliable than the TV for news when the perpetual fog is down) that the boss of America, Donald Trump, has stated publicly that he intends to have a 'relationship' with the boss of North Korea, Chinaman Kim Jong Un. This has set the proverbial cat amongst the pigeons here in Llanaber.

Mrs. T, who is planning to host their meeting on June 12th in the room for rent above her sweet shop in the high street, is not a big fan of those of the 'differently ugly-bumpers' (DUBs) persuasion. In fact, she can't stand them, despite 'those of that persuasion' being always polite and very well turned out.

So, this announcement by Trump has put her in a quandary.

Firstly, she has a sign in her shop window strictly prohibiting canoodling between same sex customers in the queue for her fudge. Admittedly there is no such prohibition notice currently on display in the room above the shop that's for rent, but knowing her, she'll probably knock up a copy of the one downstairs and pin it to the wallpaper in the room ahead of June 12th.

Secondly, there is only one table in the room and that is only 2 ft. wide. Mr. Trump and Chinaman Kim are both, let's say, a bit on the bulky side. They will inevitably be touching knees, if not guts, under such a small table. Could the fact that the table is so tiny, relative to the massive heft of the two world-leading brainiacs, be misconstrued as 'enabling' i.e. positively encouraging intimacy between the two anorexia deniers?

I know Mrs. T can't swap out the table for a larger one because the staircase up to the room is too narrow.

Finally, there is the issue of security. You can see into the room above her shop from the bus stop across the road. What if the two mega-guts started holding hands again? Or, heaven forfend, caressing?

What if they then got 'photographed?'

The worldwide maelstrom of scandal would ruin Mrs. T's impeccable reputation as a bigot and a 'no-nonsense' puritanical homophobic zealot.

Balance the above against Mrs. T's potential loss of revenue and you can see why she's in a tizzy. Admittedly she hasn't yet received the £25 deposit for the room from either party, but she has baked 600 airy-fairy cakes especially for their carousal. There isn't a snowball in hell's chance of her shifting that stock if the Trump / Kim meeting falls through again. None of the locals will touch her ghastly cakes and there are currently only six tourists in the village that might be dumb enough to buy one. These baked monstrosities (the cakes not the tourists – there's no chance of them being baked when the fog's down) should only be used as doorstops or sold to the Travelers for ammunition against the Druid's devil dogs.

To make matters even worse for Mrs. T, she has heard that Chinaman Kim is demanding accommodation to the value of $6,000 per night but can only pay in noodles. As leader of the parish council it would fall within Mrs. T's purview to ensure Chinaman Kim's needs are fully met.

But how?

The village doesn't have a hotel, let alone a posh one.

One of the village farmers, 'Ifor the sheep,' occasionally rents space for campers at the boggy end of his field, but it doesn't even come close to hygienic let alone a glamorous experience.

Old Mrs. Clinton has a room above her card shop with a bed in it. She has been known to rent this out on occasion. But it's a nonstarter because Mrs. T had her locked up by the village cop (Robbie the Bobbie) a few days ago when the two of them exposed her as a rabid left-wing anti-establishment columnist.

It's possible Mrs. T could use her powers to pardon Mrs. Clinton and let her out ahead of the carousal but that's unlikely. She's never forgiven Mrs. Clinton for standing against her in the 2016 election campaign for leader.

Also, Chinaman Kim can only pay in noodles. That, in and of itself, creates a problem. Math was never my subject, but even a dunce like me can work out there would be a storage issue. Mrs. Clinton sells cards, so her stock room is tiny. A stack of packets of noodles would occupy more space than is available in the only other space she has to store stock, i.e. her spare bedroom.

I for one am praying to the Gods that Mr. Trump's half-witted underlings, the loud-mouthed fart John Bolton and the Albino lizard Mike Pence, will start spitting again and the whole thing will be called off once and for all. If the world truly wants peace, then sack all these nincompoops and get some grown-ups to do the job, preferably women (Mrs. Trim notwithstanding).

I read that the funny (as in peculiar) lady, Samantha Bee, has bowed to pressure from 'Trump the Tweet' (as the villagers refer to him) and the US Republican party. To save her hide she has now apologized for calling Mr. Trump's thin grinner of a daughter, Wanka, a 'feckless (insert expletive here).'

Quite right too!

Wanka is NOT feckless. She found one of the 1,500 missing Mexican kids, didn't she? That's more than the waspish Samantha Bee has ever done.

And as to the vile rude word used by Bee about the thin grinner, it's cruel and totally unjustified. Wanka can't help that. It's hereditary.

That's it for now.

Cheerio!

TRUMP'S PARDON FOR TRUMP MAY SET PRECEDENT

I have previously reported that the amber faced super-hero and brainiac, Donald Trump, is going around saying 'pardon' to rather a lot of his pals at the moment, but it could get even more bizarre. A fascinating piece of information came through on the village ticker tape this morning. Apparently in the US, the boss of America's attorney, the consigliore from the Godfather, Rudy Giuliani, is going about telling all and sundry that will listen to the bulky bit part player that President Trump has the power to pardon himself.

I've destroyed this section of the ticker tape news feed. I've filled in the gap in the tape with a recipe for Bara Brith (a lump of rock made from bread ingredients and sawdust popular with the villagers). I don't want Mrs. Trim, the boss of the village council here, getting wind of this little ruse. She'd adopt this power into the village council constitution in a flash. Then she'd go and beat the crap out of poor old Mrs. Clinton, the old girl that runs the card shop in the village. Mrs. Clinton's currently residing in the village clink after an 'Arkady Babchenco' style sting pulled off by Mrs. T. This exposed old mother Clinton as a filthy and lefty subversive for wanting to drag Mrs. T's fat kids back off their 'fact finding' trip to Disney Orlando at the village's expense. No doubt Mrs. T, after having beaten poor Mrs. Clinton, would grant herself a pardon. This would be a step too far in any democracy, let alone the one in Llanaber, and set a very worrying, democracy threatening precedent.

Now that 'Trump the Tweet' (as the villagers call him) and Chinaman Kim are going to have their well-publicized spitting contest (hopefully here in Llanaber), a special Trump / Kim commemorative coin is going to be produced in the US and put on sale. Never one to let a profit-making opportunity go stale, Mrs. T plans to nick the idea and bake a Trump / Kim commemorative batch of airy-fairy cakes and put them on sale in her sweet shop window before, during and after the historic carousal in the room for rent above her shop.

Each individual cake will have a life-sized effigy of Mr. Trump's head on one side and Chinaman Kim's head on the other, face to face, both eyeballing each other menacingly. These are going to be very wide cakes as both men have heads bigger than soccer balls. Mrs. T has diverted funds away from the village hospital to finance the enlargement of her shop window.

Whilst official tenders for the proposed extension work have been issued and returned, I'm confident the contract will go to Mrs. T's preferred supplier of building services, her husband, Leonard. This is in spite of his bid being ten times the cost of that of the next most expensive.

This brings me to another point. I note with some regret that Mrs. T has not yet filled the vacancy for the recently proposed new position on the council for a village 'Anti-Corruption and Nepotism Tsar.' Llanaber, like the US, is desperately in need of someone to do this job. At least in the US Mr. Trump has dependable people he can call upon to fill such a vacancy, Jared Kushner for example, or perhaps Trump's upright young son, fun-sized Donald Jr.

Speaking of Jared, it came through on the ticker tape that the lad's father, real estate magnate Charles Kushner, is getting a little hot under the collar with the federal ethics watchdogs who have been hounding him and his delightful thin son. It has been reported that old Mr. K has called them 'jerks who can't get a real job.'

I for one agree with Mr. Kushner (Sr.). He is right, and I have the proof. When I heard what the shy, retiring old chap said I carried out a straw poll in the village. I set up a stand not too near the ever-widening sink hole in the middle of the road in the main street. I then invited the villagers clinging to the walls as they skirted the hole to answer two simple questions as follows:

1. What is a real estate magnate?
2. What is a federal ethics watchdog?

Whilst some of the answers were a little on the bizarre side (some villagers confused a magnate with a magnet), by far and away the majority of those polled understood clearly what a real estate magnate was.

However, when asked what a federal ethics watchdog was, I have to report there was no such clear understanding. Most people thought it was a breed of Alsatian guard dog, the sort you see chained up in scrap yards. I therefore can only conclude that being a federal ethics watchdog is <u>not</u> a real job, and what the humble, self-deprecating wizened old plutocrat said is correct. If Mr. K senior wants to be hounded then at least let it be by folks with a proper job, like the FBI for example.

I see from the village ticker tape that the Democrats in the US are blaming poor old beleaguered Mr. Trump for US fuel prices cresting $3 per gallon now. What is it with the Democrats? He's damned if he does and he's damned if he doesn't with these guys! They wanted Donald Trump not to pull out of the Kyoto protocol to 'stop the planet from getting a bit warmer.' Now they're moaning because Trump wants to reduce carbon dioxide emissions by making driving a luxury beyond the pocket of the poor and the majority of blue collar Americans.

You can't have it both ways!

That said, I for one am in favor of the increased emission of carbon dioxide in the US if it helps lift the perpetual fog that blights our village.

That's it for now.

Cheerio!

PARDON FRENZY 'MAY HIT LLANABER' FEARS

I'm getting more and more concerned that Mrs. Trim will hear the stories coming out of the US about the boss of America, Donald Trump, and his bizarre thinking on presidential pardons. I've been up all night burning the relevant sections of ticker tape that I've cut out of the village news feed in case she sees them.

I'm confused myself, and it doesn't help that 'Trump the Tweet's' lawyer, the consigliore from the Godfather, Rudi Giuliani, keeps sticking his beak in with a new version of Trump's opinion every five minutes.

Nevertheless, it is my responsibility as village Foreign Secretary to get my head round these complicated issues, so I can make an informed assessment of what's going on in that empty barn of a brain of the leader of the free world.

So, here goes.

Donald Trump believes that as President of the US he has the absolute right to pardon himself for things he has 'done wrong.' It's not just his opinion, but also the opinion of many of his friends that he has recently pardoned, his consigliore, Giuliani, and a few batty professors of law that will sell their legal opinion on anything for fifty bucks and a free round of golf.

Okay so far if true. My problem comes with what Mr. Trump also said, and I quote his tweet on the subject verbatim below:

"As has been stated by numerous legal scholars, I have the absolute right to PARDON myself, but why would I do that when I have done nothing wrong?"

My issue is this. If a person can pardon themselves when they do something wrong and the said pardon absolves them for having done something wrong, then by definition, at the end of the process they have done nothing wrong.

Have they?

If my reasoning is correct, whatever that person did, by definition, can NEVER be wrong when pardoned. So, that person could fill his back yard with puppies and drive a steam roller over the lot of them, then pardon himself, then go buy more puppies with a clear conscience.

That, in and of itself, is frightening enough, but what if said person just happened to be a narcissistic, thin-skinned, egotistical, racist, lying, bigoted, nepotistic, misogynist, who had the biggest nuclear arsenal on the planet at his fingertips? (Hypothetically – I'm not thinking about anyone specifically here).

Pretty scary, eh, but not half as scary as is would become here if Mrs. T got hold of the idea. We'd have to smuggle old Mrs. Clinton out of the village for a start (if we could spring her from the jail). Also, I would have great concerns about the village hospital budget, or what little is left of it. There's just enough money remaining in this year's pot to carry out ten more candlelit operations, or to pay for a soft furnishing refurbishment of Mrs. T's parlor. I'll keep burning ticker tape in the hope the money's spent on the former, not the latter.

The village council meeting last night did not go well. There were scenes. You may recall that accusations were flying around the village following the 2016 election for council leader. This was a 'two horse' race between Mrs. T and old Mrs. Clinton that runs the card shop. The accusations were that the election was 'nobbled' by the chap that runs the amusement arcade on the seafront, the 'beast from the east,' Putin Lotzadosh. He was accused of offering free goes on the penny falls machines in his arcade to those entitled to vote, i.e. shop owners and concessionaires for the bouncy castle and donkey rides on the beach.

The village cop, Robert (Robbie the Bobbie) Muller, is due to publish the findings of his investigation very soon. There was uproar in the chamber when Mrs. T demanded to see a copy of the Muller report ahead of publication. Her justification is that she needs to check the text for spelling mistakes, and I quote Mrs. T verbatim,

"Because Robbie's Eng. Lang & Lit. were never his strong subjects."

What were? He's as dumb as a brick (where have I heard that phrase before?).

Mrs. T's demand is unprecedented, out of order, and smacks of perversion of justice. Why? Because I fear she may 'doctor' the report. She has been known to do this in the past.

As part of her obligations on becoming council leader she was required to publish her tax returns in full. This she refused to do, her reasoning being, and again I quote her words verbatim, "It's none of your bleedin' business!"

After much legal wrangling between the council's legal team and Mrs. T's lawyer, the amateur video enthusiast and pervert, Solly Weinstein (no relation), Mrs. T agreed to publish a redacted version. This turned out to be a sheet of paper painted black.

The improvements to Mrs. T's shop window have been completed at the village hospital's budget's expense. Despite the ridiculous cost of the upgrade, I must confess the widened frontage of her shop looks great. The first of Mrs. T's commemorative Trump / Kim airy-fairy cakes is now proudly on display in the new shop window. While I was standing in front of the shop admiring Mrs. T's handy work a tourist came and stood next to me. I asked him for his opinion.

"Looks like two fucking huge orange soccer balls with ugly faces painted on, just about to spit at each other," he said.

The man had got it wrong. He was looking at a large poster of the American commemorative Trump / Kim coin that Mrs. T has put in the window as a backdrop.

"Not the poster," I said, "The cake!"

"Looks like two fucking huge orange soccer balls with ugly faces painted on, just about to spit at each other in 3D," he said.

That's it for now.

Cheerio!

CELEBRATION OF LLANABER EVENT 'GOES PEAR!'

I think Mrs. Trim, the idiot that's the boss of the Llanaber village council, has completely lost her marbles. The entire council were red faced and bewildered by the on goings in the council chamber yesterday. I suspect there may be a move made soon to approach Dr. Mengele, the chap that runs the village hospital, to see if we can have her sectioned. We have a secret code word we used when discussing whether to have the mad old bat locked up. We got it from the Americans. Instead of saying that we're going to have Mrs. T 'sectioned under the Mental Health Act 1983,' we simply say
'impeached.'

Let me give you the background.

The village has a rugby team, the 'Llanaber Lard-asses.' This is principally made up from fourteen of the fattest lads from the village plus a little whippet of a lad that's just joined called Mervin 'Merve the Swerve' Evans. Those that are unfamiliar with the game of rugby won't know how it's played so I'll briefly give you an outline. Two teams face each other on a muddy field. A ball is involved somehow. They run around in the perpetual fog for eighty minutes shouting out, trying to find each other, then go to the pub and get hammered. It's a game for men, women, and children, and is very popular in Wales.

There is a 'Welsh Villages League' that has a final every year between the best two teams. The Llanaber Lard-asses won this event for the first time in the village's history. Merve the Swerve was the 'man of the match' having actually found the ball in the fog.

Now I come to the crux of the story.

When the news of our team's victory came through on the ticker tape, Mrs. T unilaterally decided to divert funds from the village hospital's budget into putting on a celebratory shindig for the returning heroes of the rugby team. I say returning because the final was held in Druidellau. The Druids are the only ones in the area with enough money for a pitch. They rent this out to other villages but insist that both teams sign a form supporting the Druids' use of devil dogs to oppress the Travelers, and that one of the Traveler's kids is used instead of the ball.

Our victorious team was expected back in Llanaber at 3pm on the day of the match. Mrs. T had baked a special commemorative batch of her airy-fairy cakes, and an urn full of tea was brewed. The council members were ordered to put on their smartest togs and stand around in the council chambers looking as if they cared. All was set for the great event. Mrs. T had even named the event her 'Celebration of Llanaber.'

To cut a long story short, the team refused to attend. They had gotten wind that Mrs. T's lawyer and amateur pervert, Solly Weinstein (no relation), had been given some money from Mrs. T to make a video of their homecoming. Further, Solly was insisting that all the players pose naked.

The outcome was that the team cried off. The team captain, 'Evans the Punt' later told the village newsletter, "We never asked for a party so why should we go down on one knee to her over this?"

The team's reaction is understandable if you see it from the players' point of view. They hadn't showered after the match. Also, with the exception of 'Merve the Swerve,' the members of the team are all chubby lads. Most importantly of all, on the day of the match it was bitterly cold. I'll say no more.

If the village maidens had gotten hold of the video, let's just say 'reputations may have been damaged.'

Instead of attending Mrs. T's bash, the lads took the bus to Spanibont. There they piled into the 'Abandon All Hope' pub in the high street, got drunk, then had their traditional 'after match fight' with the rowdies.

Mrs. T was left looking red-faced at the empty stage in the council chambers, i.e. the half a dozen pallets hastily nailed together for the homecoming heroes by Leonard, Mrs. T's better half.

She went apoplectic!

When she found out they had turned down her kind offer she stepped onto the stage, wrapped herself in the Welsh flag, then sang 'Bread of Heaven' for twenty minutes at maximum lung capacity. When she had finished singing, she spread her arms out to the near empty room and proclaimed, "This is a beautiful big celebration."

Surely the mad old hag can't keep her job much longer! I haven't checked the news ticker tape this morning but let's hope Donald Trump's 'Celebration of America' went a little more smoothly than Mrs. T's effort, and that The Philadelphia Eagles all had a wonderful time in the White House.

The latest on the village ticker tape news feed is that President Macron, the boss of France, has been quoted as saying his reportedly 'terrible' phone call to Donald Trump about the boss of America's great idea to unilaterally apply tariffs to steel imports, is like sausages: 'better not explain what's inside.'

Who does this diminutive Frenchy think he is?

The village butcher, 'Evans the Pork,' is very proud of his sausages and has no shame in publishing the recipe, which I now do in full, although the exact proportions of ingredients must remain a secret as this information is of commercial sensitivity:

'Beef fat, emulsified pork fat, pork jowls, mechanically reformed pork trim, ice, salt, phosphate, sodium nitrate, sodium nitrite, sodium erythorbate, artificial pepper substitute, monosodium glutamate, sawdust, collagen sleeve sausage skin substitute.'

Having re-read the recipe, Macron may have a point about sausages, but you can't knock Mr. Trump's idea of a 25% tariff on imported steel. Blue collar workers have it hard enough in the US as it is. Choking off manufacturing companies' low-cost steel supply will undoubtedly impinge on production and give these lower income blue collar workers a well-earned break when their factories go out of business.

That's it for now.

Cheerio!

MEMORIAL DAY HI-JACKED BY EGO BABBLE

There has been more scandal in the village regarding the ever increasingly outrageous behavior of our esteemed leader, Mrs. Trim, the boss of the parish council. It was Memorial Day in Llanaber yesterday, always a somber event. On such occasions, traditionally, a wreath is laid on the village Cenotaph by the council boss, a few words are said to the assembled praising the heroic sacrifice made by the fallen, then we all go to the pub for commemorative drinks and food. Not so this year with Mrs. T at the helm.

Here's what happened.

Firstly, ahead of the event, Mrs. T diverted a significant wedge of cash from the village hospital budget into what she referred to as her 'Memorial Day slush fund.' The money is to be used for her and her chubby-hubby, Leonard, to go on a fact-finding tour of Cenotaphs in the Bahamas during the winter months to 'study cultural differences' regarding the celebration of the fallen.

Then she scrapped the idea of a wreath, replacing it with a commemorative 'basket of airy-fairy cakes.' These turned out to be the 'out of code' cakes she'd foolishly baked too far ahead of the Trump / Kim carousal, due to take place in the room above her shop. They are now past their 'best before' date. We've had a long run of perpetual fog lying on the village recently, and that knocks the bejeezus out of the shelf life of Mrs.T's cakes. It was a <u>massive</u> basket. There were 600 cakes. Mrs. T's airy-fairy cakes have a density greater than lead. It took the whole of the rugby team, the Llanaber Lardies, to lift the bloody thing up the Cenotaph steps.

To add insult to injury Mrs. T charged the village £100 per cake! She only charges the foolish and tourists £2 a cake when she sells them in her shop.

But worse was to come. I am referring here to her speech.

What should have been a few kind words about the fallen turned into a mixture of a polemic, an advert for her shop, and a self-congratulatory assessment of her performance as the Parish Council Chair since she took office in 2016.

The polemic was, of course, aimed at poor old Mrs. Clinton, the old girl that runs the card shop in the high street who is currently residing in the village clink after being 'outed' as a commie subversive in an Arkady Babchenco style sting. Mrs. T ran on for half an hour about the poor old girl, repeatedly demanding that our top-cop, Robert 'Robbie the Bobbie' Muller, brushes the cobwebs off his D.I.Y. waterboarding kit and gives Mrs. C 'what for.'

It got worse.

Mrs. T then produced sheets of paper with a price list of 'special offers' from her sweet shop and insisted everyone 'pay homage to the fallen' via the medium of sweet eating. I couldn't see how stuffing our faces with confectionery celebrated the sacrifices these people made for the village, and rather stupidly raised this point with Mrs. T.

I should have kept my face shut. I repeat below verbatim what Mrs. T's response was:

"Shut your hole, you skinny idiot! These heroes sacrificed everything for the village. The least we can do is raise a celebratory lump of fudge to their memory!"

Then she continued as follows, "If they were alive today they'd be proud of what I've achieved since my election in 2016. They'd look at my sweet shop window and say, 'Wow!' They'd look at the ever-widening sink hole in the high street and be proud that I have at last found a safe place to get rid of the village garbage. They'd look at the excellent work I'm doing to reconcile the Druids and the Travelers by siding with the Travelers... Only joking, siding with the Druids, obviously. They'd congratulate me in my visionary strategic thinking in calling on the villagers in Spanibont to erect a fence at their expense to keep their rowdies out of Llanaber. They'd..." and blah, blah, blah!

She ran on for another hour, the big headed old crow.

At least Donald Trump, when he hi-jacked the US Memorial Day event with his self-effacing assessment of his own modest achievements since taking office, had the decency to do it in a short speech followed up with a tweet!

People can be cruel. The perpetual fog lifted last night and I saw on the TV that the cheese ball colored Brainiac who is the boss of America, Donald Trump, was saying kind words about his thin, 'lingerie model potential' wife, Melanie at her first public appearance since her gastric band operation. There have been some unpleasant, and in some cases, downright scurrilous rumors about why Melanie has been off the scene for so long. Below are examples:

· She's a robot and the brain bit malfunctioned. They couldn't get the spare they needed from Russia.
· Her facelift operation went wrong and there were signs of pubic hairs on her neck.

    ·   Donald left her in a cupboard in the
White House and forgot which one.
And the most outrageous of them all,
    ·   Donald Trump had beaten her when
she asked why he'd taken $130,000 from her
housekeeping and given it to Michael Cohen.

The appearance of the amber faced comb-over and his good lady sitting side by side at the Federal Emergency Management Agency has finally put an end to these 'unfair and vicious' rumors. The President spoke warmly of and for his wife throughout the booze up. Unfortunately, Melanie was unable to talk as her jaws were wired together.

That's it for now.

Cheerio!

GIULIANI HOMO-EROTIC COMMENTS ABOUT KIM THREATENS LLANABER SUMMIT

Salon.com - Former New York City Mayor Rudolf Giuliani introduces Republican presidential nominee Donald Trump at a campaign rally in Greenville, North Carolina, U.S., September 6, 2016. REUTERS/Mike Segar - RTX2OEXW

There was yet another furious outburst in the council meeting last night from our village boss, Mrs. Trim. This time her vitriolic rant was aimed at Donald Trump's lawyer, the bulky chap that played the consigliore in the Godfather, Rudy Giuliani. In this case I must confess I agreed with every acid coated word that spattered from my esteemed leader's lips.

Is this guy Giuliani as dumb as a brick? (Where have I heard that phrase before?)

No sooner is the carousal back on between the two-massive brainiacs and anorexia deniers, President Trump and Chinaman Kim, when one of Trump's half-witted loud mouthed subordinates starts another spitting contest with the North Koreans.

You will recall last time the whole shindig was called off because of rooftop crowing from Mr. Trump's cretinous also-rans, the loud-mouthed fart Bolton and the Albino lizard Pence. Poor old Mr. Trump had to write his humiliating 'as if I'm bothered' open letter to try and coax the soccer-ball skulled lad back to the meeting table.

What these idiots don't understand is that Chinaman Kim Jong Un is at a sensitive age and has only recently 'come out.' It doesn't take much social media bullying before he'll be running back to his bedroom, locking the door to the world and mithering over the curse of his sexual orientation.

So, what has the melting-faced consigliore said that has put in jeopardy the meeting scheduled for June 12th in the room for rent above Mrs. Trim's shop?

Giuliani has boasted that after the meeting was canceled last time, and I quote the Godfather bit player verbatim here:

"Kim Jong-un got back on his hands and knees and 'begged for it,' which is exactly the position you want to put him in." Outrageous!

Pervy Giuliani should keep his homo-erotic fantasies to himself!

Doesn't he realize that Chinaman Kim is already in a 'relationship' with his 'new pal' from down south, the boss of South Korea, Moon Jae-in? Has Giuliani been living on the moon (no relation)? Didn't he see the extensive media coverage when Kim Jong Un and Moon Jae-in 'got papped' when caught openly holding hands in public?

If consigliore Giuliani fancies Chinaman Kim and 'wants to see him on his hands and knees begging for it' then he should not voice his homo-erotic fantasies openly.

Be a Man! Take a box of tissues to the men's restroom and get it out of your system once and for all, for Chrissake!

You might think of Kim as eye candy, but he's more than just a sex object. Try and see beyond the boyish good looks and seductively curvy figure.

Think of the potential consequences if this meeting is cancelled yet again.

Mrs. T has already baked 600 Trump / Kim commemorative airy-fairy cakes, especially for the meeting. If those big buggers go stale they set like concrete. We'd have to pay the Llanaber Lardies, the village rugby team, to roll them out of her shop and into the sink hole in the high street. What's more, the lads will want a bung for doing such heavy work, and I fear there are insufficient funds left in the village hospital budget to cover the cost.

I was astounded by a piece of news that came through on the village ticker tape yesterday. A US State Department spokeswoman, Ms. Heather Nauert (is that a German name?) was quoted as saying the following:

"Looking back in the history books, today is the 71st anniversary of the speech that announced the Marshall Plan. Tomorrow is the anniversary of the D-Day invasion. We obviously have a very long history with the government of Germany, and we have a strong relationship with the government of Germany"

However, it wasn't Ms. Nauert's statement that astounded me. Some old retired fuddy-duddy called Malcolm Nance switched back on his life support machine for a few minutes and spat out that Ms. Nauert was, and I quote him verbatim:

"Disgracefully ignorant of the 'relationship' with Hitler's Nazi
Germany at Normandy 74 years ago today. Quit now. Its 7th
grade history." Is he a complete nitwit?

Ms. Nauert quite correctly pointed out that the US and Germany shared an especially bonding piece of history back then, inasmuch that they spent rather a lot of time firing bits of metal at each other with intent to maim and kill. Such shared experiences will undoubtedly lead to the forming of tight bonds, usually of the splints and bandages kind.

That said, it is unfair to compare the warmth and closeness shared between the US and Germany back in 1946 to the relationship between the two countries now. These days America's ruling political class has shifted much more to the right, and the Germans now try to dump their steel on Americans in the form of container ships full of cut priced girders as opposed to white hot shrapnel.

That's it for now.

Cheerio.

CALL FOR PUTIN'S RETURN TO TABLE PUTS LLANABER IN UPROAR

The amazing outburst by the cheese-ball faced anorexia denier, Donald Trump, has set the cat amongst the pigeons here in Llanaber big style. When 'Trump the Tweet' made his 'out of left field' statement that his alleged backers & hackers, Russia, should be at the G7 meeting Mrs. Trim jumped straight on the bandwagon with both feet. We had hardly settled in our seats in the village council chamber when Mrs. T stood up and demanded that an extra chair be brought into the chamber and put next to hers at the head of the table. I stupidly asked why. She gave me one of her withering looks and then spoke to me as if I was an idiot.

"For Putin," she said, barely disguising her annoyance.

There was a sharp intake of breath from all the other council members.

Why?

Because Putin Lotzadosh, the 'beast from the east' that owns the slot machine arcade on the sea front, has been persona non-grata in the village with all but Mrs. T since 2016.

There is strong anecdotal evidence to suggest that baldy bonce Putin (the bear with no hair) nobbled the 2016 election to the benefit of Mrs. T. This he did by offering those entitled to a vote free goes on the Penny Falls machines in his arcade.

Whilst there is not yet any irrefutable evidence in the public domain, there is an on-going investigation being carried out into the matter by Robert 'Robbie the Bobbie' Muller, the village cop. His report is due anytime now but has to be 'vetted' by Mrs. T before release. This, she has assured us, is necessary to 'correct Robbie's terrible grammar and any spelling mistakes,' and is a task she has given her word will be undertaken without interference with, or showing any bias for or against, the report's conclusions.

The delay in releasing 'The Muller Report' is because 'Robbie the Bobbie' and his wife have been sent by Mrs. T, using funds diverted from the village hospital budget, on a fact-finding tour of bars and restaurants in the Florida Keys. This is so he can fully assess the differences in food and drink quality between the US and Llanaber, and the effects of alcohol poisoning on a person collapsing comatose on the beach in a sunny environment as opposed to that of perpetual fog.

Until the report into Putin's electoral activities is published, and Putin is either exonerated or banged up in the village prison, it is an unwritten rule amongst the members of the council chamber that Putin is to be ignored by all.

So, Mrs. T's demand for the 'slot machine Slav' to now have a seat at the table before the report is out, is a blow for those who believe in democracy, justice, and free and fair elections.

FYI – We live in a thriving democracy in Llanaber so, to keep it that way, voting rights are restricted here to only the villagers of substance, i.e. those who either own shops in the high street or run the donkey and bouncy castle concessions on the beach. We don't want any old person casting votes for any idiot they want and ruining it for those of us with some money in the bank.

I have suspicions that there may be more to Mrs. T's desire to have the 'beast from the east' readmitted into polite society than the matter of the Muller report alone. I know Putin made an approach to the parish council to buy a plot of swampy marsh near the estuary called Bogbourne. This was quite rightly turned down. There is a lot of retired folk living in wooden huts on stilts in the marshes there, and Putin wanted to get shot of them to make space to store his collection of life sized models of battleships, missiles and tanks. I've subsequently heard the sound of sawing late into the night coming from Bogbourne, and counted a lot fewer huts on stilts lately. Also, I've seen Putin's henchmen wrapped in Clingfilm going up to the doors of these huts and spreading an 'unknown substance' on the mail boxes.

I suspect mischief from the 'baldy Balkan.'

I wouldn't put it past him to take matters into his own hands, defy the council and annex this outlying area of the village to his slot machine arcade empire. This would be a disaster. Apart from it being mega-illegal, what would the council do if we lost this boggy, mosquito ridden swamp? Where would we put all of the 'out of datecode' villagers until they kick the bucket? We neither have the budget nor a graveyard in the village to bury these destitute old codgers.

We need that quicksand!

That's it for now.

Cheerio!

LLANABER DEFENDS TRUMP'S SLOBBER ON KELLY CRAFT

There were ugly rumors flying around the village last night about the quiet, self-deprecating boss of America, Donald Trump's potentially lascivious behavior again. The vicious character assassinating tittle-tattle concerned an 'awkward moment' that occurred when Mr. Trump gave diplomat and 'lingerie model potential' hottie, Kelly Knight Craft, an inept French style hello.

As the Foreign Secretary for Llanaber village council, I've been ordered by the boss of the village, Mrs. Dorothy 'Binky' Trim, to investigate the matter and find out what really happened.

Why? (I hear you ask).

Because Mrs. T will jump on any old bandwagon that Mr. Trump is riding on. If it's now 'de rigueur' to paw at any dignitaries that visit our village, she wants in on the act straight away! She has a little of the Monica Lewinski in her and gets frisky when in the presence of powerful men.

The perpetual fog is lying thick on the village now so I'm unable to get hold of a clip of the actual event. However, the stories in the village range from "It was a bit of a clumsy kiss" through "He was all slobber and she vomited," right up to "His tongue was at the back of her throat when he copped a feel of her left tit."

No doubt the truth will lie somewhere between these extremes, but my faith will not be shaken in Mr. Trump's impeccable track record when it comes to respecting a lady's physical boundaries. That said, I do hope this little incident doesn't mean his plastic-faced gastric banded wife, Melanie, doesn't lose another $130,000 from her housekeeping for a secret bribe to the lady involved.

It is not easy to get right a friendly, non-sexual greeting of an acquaintance or stranger with a French style light kiss on the cheeks. I know I've bumped foreheads and got my spectacles entangled with awkwardly dangling earrings in the past. I also know it happens to other American politicians too, so Donald Trump shouldn't feel embarrassed. Mr. Trump has a fragile ego and is prone to shyness and sulking if he thinks he's done something stupid. We don't want him withdrawing to his bedroom for a sulk when he has an important meeting ahead of him. Here I refer, of course, not to the current G7 (6 in one room and Trump in another) meeting, but to his forthcoming carousal with the chubby DUB* lad, the boss of North Korea, scheduled for June 12th at Mrs. T's shop.

How do I know these awkward French style 'moa-moas' happen to other American politicians? (I hear you ask yet again).

I saw a campaign video by Maryland's Democratic gubernatorial candidate Rich Madaleno in which he repeatedly praises Donald Trump, saying, "Take that

Trump!" – I assume he meant "Take (as in 'How about') that Trump, eh? What a great guy!"

Anyway, at the end of the video he leant forward and accidentally bumped his mouth against the lips of some other chap that happened to be sitting next to him. This must have been an awkward moment for them both as it could appear to someone with a twisted mind that the two men kissed.

See! Mistakes like this can easily happen, Mr. Trump, so chin up, eh?

I've heard rumors that Donald Trump's 2019 budget could cut spending for the Mental Health Administration by $665 million, and slash funding for the National Institute of Mental Health by 30 percent. People that are a little on the bonkers side needn't lose heart. Mr. Trump's thin grinner of a daughter, Wanka, is doing her bit to help her Dad. After the tragic death of Kate Spade, Wanka tweeted, and I quote verbatim here:

"Kate Spade's tragic passing is a painful reminder that we never truly know another's pain or the burden they carry. If you are struggling with depression and contemplating suicide, please, please seek help."

I understand she then got togged up in Spades posh clobber and pranced about a bit for the cameras. Well done little lady. No wonder your Dad is so proud of you.

By 'please, seek help' I assume she meant seek help to top yourself.

Through actively seeking out those that facilitate assisted suicides you are doing your bit to make America great again. Even the demise of a single individual that's mentally fruit-loop will be a small contribution towards reducing the overall number of depressed and suicidal people in the US, thus taking a little pressure off the 'soon to be drastically reduced' mental health budget. It would also cheer the rest of us up not to have your long face moping about, blubbing and seeking attention all the time.

Llanaber has been wrestling with the problem of how to improve care for the mentally challenged in the village for many years, but now we think we have that problem finally cracked (no pun intended).

The village council takes its obligations extremely seriously as far as the treatment of those afflicted with 'fizzy brain' is concerned. This term of endearment is used by the locals to refer to the one ding-bat in our village who happens to be a Gene short of his DNA's full quota. I refer, of course, to old fizzy brain, Willie 'the Window Licker' Clinton. He is the estranged husband of Mrs. Clinton, the lady that runs the card shop in the high street. He is also Llanaber's official village idiot.

True, Willie undoubtedly has mental issues. He's painted his head white as a fashion statement and goes around telling anyone who will listen that he used to run the parish council. But being deluded is no reason for the old chap not to stand on his own two feet in society like any other less barmy citizen.

In our village we believe in 'care in the community.' Despite Willie being a fully qualified 'nut job' (where have I heard that phrase before?) the council has given the old codger rent-free accommodation in 'mad man's corner.' This is a tent set up at the bottom of 'Ifor the sheep's' field near the boggy end, kept exclusively for those not welcomed in polite society. Also, the white headed old duffer gets paid ten pounds a week, cash in hand, plus a bag of fudge for daily licking the shop windows in the high street until they sparkle in the fog.

Mr. Trump could learn a thing or two from Llanaber's enlightened approach to the mentally challenged. Lesson number one would be to point his fun-sized son, Donald jnr., towards a career in window licking, so the lad can start contributing to US society in a more positive way than to date.

That's it for now.
Cheerio!

TRUMP NOT WELCOME IN LLANABER AFTER 'NO SEAT FOR MERKEL' SCANDAL

Outrage in Llanaber! If what we have seen coming through on the village news ticker tape is true then the village council has been massively duped by the American administration. Chinaman Kim Jong Un and his entourage have turned up in Singapore! Further, messages on the news feed indicate that the boss of America, Donald Trump, is currently sitting in his posh plane and airborne. It would appear that he is also heading towards Singapore.

What a massive con!

Everyone in the village was expecting the arrival of Chinaman Kim and President Trump in Llanaber today. Instead, we discovered that our village, and more importantly our council leader, Mrs. Dorothy 'Binky' Trim, have been part of an intricate 'double-bluff.' It's like being in one of those extremely tedious books by John Le Carre about his fictional spying chap, Smiley, but for real.

Who can we now trust if not the current American administration?

Let me briefly remind you of the background:

When the news of a potential Trump / Kim spitting contest was first on the cards, Mrs. T offered the US administration the use of the room for rent above her shop on the main street from 2pm for one hour on June 12ᵗʰ. The American government agreed terms and a check for £25 was sent to Mrs. T to secure the room.

Within moments of the meeting being agreed, Mr. Trump's cretinous loser, loud-mouthed fart Bolton and Albino lizard Pence started crowing so Chinaman Kim pulled the plug. The US administration made overtures to Mrs. T to try and get their £25 deposit back but she remained resolute and banked the check.

A deal is a deal, and <u>Donald Trump is nothing if not a man of his word</u>, the 1992 United Nations Framework Convention on Climate Change, and the Iranian Joint Comprehensive Plan of Action, G7 Summit Statement, NAFTA, agreed Steel & Aluminum Tariffs with Mexico, Canada and the EU, $130,000 payoff to Stormy Daniels, and his marriage vows notwithstanding.

Mrs. T, in a fit of pique, phoned up Benjy Yahoo, the boss of the Druids and offered the room to him for his 'let's kiss and make up' meeting with the Travelers.

FYI – These meetings never actually take place. The Druids turn up and sit there for an hour eating Simnel cake then issue a press release that they were prepared to talk but the Travelers didn't even have the decency to turn up. The Travelers, for their part, issue a press release saying they would have loved to turn up but couldn't as they'd been kept prisoners on the sand dune they've been corralled into for the last 100 years by the Druids' henchmen and their devil dogs.

Also FYI - Whilst the Druids NEVER pay a deposit (they are a tribe that is very careful with money) Mrs. T and Benjy had an 'understanding' that a reservation had been made.

Then, literally moments after the Trim / Yahoo 'understanding,' the amber colored comb-over, brainiac and anorexia denier Donald Trump wrote his 'as if I care' open letter to the soccer ball headed lad to try to win him round.

The ploy worked. It was back on.

Mrs. T immediately gave Benjy the heave-ho (something she would never normally do because she's as thick as thieves with the Druids). A second check for £25 from the US administration duly arrived in the post for the deposit to secure the room.

Mrs. T was extremely excited, and a special batch of Trump / Kim commemorative airy-fairy cakes were baked then put on display in her enlarged shop window.

Accommodation to the equivalent value of $6,000 per night (to be paid by the Koreans in noodles) was arranged for Kim et al. for the spare room above Mrs. Clinton's card shop. The room was even given a deep clean especially for the occasion (clean sheets, the works!).

Mrs. T had also arranged for entertainment after the meeting. This was in the form of a hand-in-hand stroll along the beach for Trump and Kim (perpetual fog permitting) to watch a display of traditional Travelers' beatings, and the hunting of Travelers' kids with devil dogs, put on by the Druids.

Now this.

Betrayal!

Mrs. T has retired to her rooms with the vapors and hasn't been seen in the village all day. I fear being the victim of such double-dealing skulduggery from the otherwise 100% trustworthy Donald Trump has shattered her faith in the honesty of politicians.

As village Foreign Secretary I have been ordered to deal with any repercussions so as none of this reflects badly on our village. Mrs. T doesn't want the world to see us as a bunch of backwater inbreds that are each as dumb as a brick (where *have* I heard that phrase before?). Plus, she wants to get her retaliation in first.

A brave face must be put on for the sake of the village.
So, here goes:
Llanaber Parish Council - General
Press Release Sunday, 10 June 2018:
17:01 (British Fog Time).

"Head of Parish Council Pulls The Plug on Trump / Kim Llanaber Summit:

At 14:00 BFT today Mrs. Dorothy 'Binky' Trim, head of the Llanaber Parish Council, made an urgent phone call to President of the United States, Donald J Trump. The purpose was to unilaterally cancel the reservation Mr. Trump had made for the room above her shop, 'Nanny Trim's Sweets 'N' Stuff, a reservation that had been secured for the upcoming summit between the oppressive dictator and Chinaman Kim.

The reason given by Mrs. Trim was her shock and ignominy at Trump's behavior at the recent G7 meeting in Canada between some world leaders, we think six, and Mr. Trump.

The council leader has issued the following statement:

"The photographs taken at the meeting clearly show Mr. Trump sitting in a chair while Prince Harry's new wife, Angela Merkel was forced to stand. It is strongly rumored that the Prince and his new bride are trying to start a family. Angela may already be at the 'fingers crossed I'm late' stage of the process. By not offering her a seat while he sat there like a lump with his pot belly bouncing off the floor, he clearly demonstrated his contempt for the British people in general and our royal family in particular. This outrageous behavior is not acceptable to the citizens of Llanaber."

Mrs. Trim then concluded her statement by saying, "I do not want the likes of him and his Albino pal hanging around the shop."

No statement has yet been issued regarding the £25 deposit handed over by the US administration to secure the room, but based on recent history it is believed highly unlikely they will be able to pry the check out of Mrs. Trim's sweaty fist."

I trust the above statement will be sufficient to throw the media dogs off the scent and salvage the village's reputation.
Personally, I never believed they were coming here in the first place.
Singapore looks much less foggy than here.
That's it for now.
Cheerio!
*Differently Ugly-bumper

LLANABER FURIOUS AT TRUMP / KIM MEETING MASSIVE DOUBLE-CROSS

Source: https://thenewdaily.com.au/news/world/2018/03/12/donald-trump-north-korea-talks/

A public inquiry has been called by Mrs. Trim, the boss of the Llanaber parish council, into the goings on surrounding the Trump / Kim summit meeting and the outrageous con-trick played on Llanaber by the US administration.

You may recall the meeting was scheduled to take place in the room for rent above Mrs. T's shop in the village high street. The US government twice paid £25 deposit to secure the room. Expenses were laid out by the village council in good faith, believing the Americans were sincere in their commitment to honor the reservation.

What expenses? (I hear you ask).

Let's just say cakes were baked.

Why would the parish council have any reason to doubt for one minute that the US government's boss would not turn up? Donald Trump is not a liar and has said so himself (**the 1992 United Nations Framework Convention on Climate Change, and the Iranian Joint Comprehensive Plan of Action, G7 Summit Statement, NAFTA, agreed Steel & Aluminum Tariffs with Mexico, Canada and the EU, $130,000 bung to Stormy Daniels, and his marriage vows notwithstanding).

There was much publicity surrounding the event. The world's media had been fed a cock-and-bull story by the American administration that the two-soccer ball headed brainiacs and anorexia deniers were to have their carousal in Singapore. Even a video was produced by Harvey Weinstein (no relation), the famous movie mogul and forceps birth pervert (allegedly), to advertise the upcoming conflab.

When Donald Trump, famous for his fake news, fed this bull to the press indicating Singapore as the venue, in our eyes it was as good as confirming beyond a shadow of a doubt that the true venue would, in fact, be Llanaber.

We members of the parish council genuinely believed all the Singapore hype was just a clever ruse to throw the pesky-press-pack off the scent. While the hordes of fat drunken journos would be sitting around outside some posh hotel in Singapore polishing their camera, picking their noses and sharing their halitosis, the real meeting would be taking place in Mrs.T's shop.

As we now know it was a double bluff. We in Llanaber were duped!

It was all lies! (i.e. it was the truth).

So, Mrs. Trim has now instructed me, as the village Foreign Secretary, to carry out a full investigation into the affair (now dubbed Rent-a-Roomgate by the villagers) and to publish my findings as a matter of urgency. The objectives and boundaries of my report have been set as follows:

1.   To understand the circumstances behind the booking made for the room for rent above Mrs. T's shop and why she was so easily duped.

2.   To report the outcome of the actual meeting between President Trump and Chinaman Kim.

3.   To make sure my conclusions make Trump come across as a lying piece of shit.

I have put an enormous amount of effort into getting to the bottom of 'events' having spent all my coffee break on it this morning, and can now publish my findings in full, 'warts and all.' So here goes:

Item no. 1 – the infamous £25 x2 deposit paid by the US administration to secure the room:

It is understandable that this seemingly massive amount of money paid by the US administration to secure the room above Mrs. Trim's shop for the proposed meeting would have appeared to be 'the clincher' as far as Mrs. T / the parish council was concerned. However, my research into the subject has revealed the following facts:

The United States: - The U.S. economy remains the largest in the world at **$19.42 trillion in 2017.** The U.S. economy is 25% of the gross world product.

Llanaber: - The Llanaber economy is significantly smaller at **£12,015 in 2017** and, as such, has too many zeros to be represented in this document as a percentage of the gross world product.

Therefore, with the relative wealth of the US compared to Llanaber being so large, it is understandable that a false impression was given to Mrs. T about the value of the 2x £25 deposit paid. She thought it was a huge amount, they thought it was small.

Item no. 2 – the outcome of the actual Trump / Kim summit meeting:

The two fat blokes met, shook hands, said nice things about each other even though one is a massively cruel dictator that suppresses his people and the other is a vain, narcissistic liar that is so paranoid he turns on his friends (I'm not sure which is which). They both signed Christmas cards to each other. Kim promised to hide his nuclear weapons better, and Trump promised not to let his men hold their noisy shooting contest near Kim's house. I don't think they kissed. Mr. Trump would be wary of doing such a thing after his disastrous slobbery French 'moa-moa' with Kelly Craft.

Item no. 3 – to make sure Donald Trump comes across as a lying piece of shit.

This is the most difficult part of my report. After extensive investigations into the behavior of Donald Trump, even to the point where I put in a 'collect' call to Robert Mueller in the States (he didn't accept the call, the tight fisted sod), I can find no evidence whatsoever that the president of the United States, Donald Trump, is a lying piece of shit (** see above).

That concludes my report into what has become known internationally as the 'Llanaber / US reverse shafting.'

I know it as a fact that Mrs. T intended to invite Mr. Trump to open the new pie and knick-knacks shop on the village main street, for which she was prepared to raid the village hospital budget to the tune of $100 as a fee.
Sadly, this morning I witnessed Mrs. T tear up the letter she had written to Mr. Trump offering him 'the gig.'

The United States and Llanaber have had a 'special relationship' for many decades now. I for one pray that Mr. Trump's recent behavior towards its long and trusted ally will not sour future relations between our two great cultures.

But as of now, stuff you Trump, you baldy-comb-over, fat faced, double crossing, orange-flavored, misogynistic, self-satisfied, lying… No! I will remain professional.

I wish you nothing but good luck, Mr. Trump. But if I were you, I'd avoid Mrs. T for the next decade or so.

That's it for now.

Cheerio!

ANGRY TRUMP'S DE NIRO TWEET HARBORS DEEPER RESENTMENT

Official White House photo by Pete Souza

The world undoubtedly works in mysterious ways. There's always more to any story than meets the eye. It's only when you begin to look behind the headlines and dig deep for the truth that one will discover what's really going on.

Take for example the recent spitting contest between, old 'potty-mouth' and has-been actor, Robert De Niro, and America's shy and retiring leader, Donald Trump.

On the face of it the evidence would suggest that Mr. De Niro was grandstanding at the Tony awards in order to court the popularity of the other left wing, pinko, live-on-your-knees, wooly minded, overpaid, self-congratulatory 'luvvies' in the audience, sat stuffing their anorexic faces with tissues and clapping like primates at every anti-Trump jibe.

So what reaction did De Niro expect after blurting out his four letter 'mouth-fart' then waving his hands in the air like a Daesh suicide bomber standing at a bus stop outside a Jewish girl's school?

His remarks, quite rightly, appeared to annoy the normally modest, self– deprecating fine fellow who is the boss of America (and therefore by definition the smartest** guy over there).

Sir Isaac Newton's third law of motion states that for every action in nature there is an equal and opposite reaction. This was Mr. Trumps, and I quote his tweet verbatim:

"Robert De Niro, a very Low IQ individual, has received to* many shots to the head by real boxers in movies. I watched him last night and truly believe he may be "punch-drunk." I guess he doesn't // realize the economy is the best it's ever been with employment being at an all-time high, and many companies pouring back into our country. Wake up Punchy!"(*his grammatical error, not mine)

At first Mr. Trump's apparently thin–skinned, childish back swipe at the revered elderly De Niro would appear to fail Mr. Trump's usually high standards of politeness, fairness and probity. Also, I struggled with what I would call 'the common sense test' when applied to Mr. Trump's tweet.

This I did for the following reasons:

I understand that Mr. De Niro is an actor, right? i.e. he earns his living by 'pretending.' He is famously known for it and would appear to have had a long and distinguished career at the job, playing many and varied roles. Even a dimwit like me knows that an actor 'pretends.'

It follows that if Mr. De Niro was playing the part of a boxer, he wouldn't actually <u>be</u> boxing. He would be <u>pretending to box</u>. As such he wouldn't (or shouldn't) knocked out.

So why then Mr. Trump's remarks? The normally infallible fanny-magnet and brainiac appeared to have 'got it wrong.'

For the avoidance of doubt I looked up the word 'acting' in the dictionary. It is both a noun and an adjective:

114

Noun: the art or occupation of performing fictional roles in plays, films, or television.

Adjective: temporarily doing the duties of another person.

When I read the two distinctly different uses the word can be put to, the perpetual fog was lifted from my mind.

I understood (or at least I thought I did).

The explanation is thus: Mr. Trump must believe Mr. De Niro is an actor in the <u>adjective</u> sense of the word. By this I mean, say, in the movie 'Raging Bull,' Mr. De Niro is 'temporarily standing in' for Jake LaMotta in an actual boxing match. In which case, De Niro would have gotten his head battered. You see actors aren't used to being professional boxers. They aren't really trained for it. Ask De Niro to sit about 'waiting for Godot' and he's in his element, but shove him in a cage with Eric 'Butterbean' Esch for five minutes, then my money would be a) on the fat lad winning and b) on Mr. De Niro pooing his pants.

So, enigma sorted. The US top-dog simply got it wrong.

But then I thought of Mr. Trump's infallibility, and his 'Garry Kasparovian' strategic three dimensional thinking mega-brain. It must be more than a simple misunderstanding of the use of a word that had gotten the cheese-ball faced anorexia denier so riled.

Think like the president, I thought to myself, see the bigger picture.

This I did.

It was so obvious. I felt such a fool for not spotting it straight away.

The President's enmity towards the full time 'pretending-to-be-somebody-else-for-a-living-and-making-$millions' De Niro had nothing to do with the actor's embarrassing claptrap at the Tony awards. Mr. Trump, like a seventy-year-old Stilton, is very mature and too thick skinned to be rattled by a dumb crowd pleasing stunt such as De Niro's.

I now believe it is as follows: Mr. Trump is ambivalent towards De Niro. He couldn't give a fly-away comb-over what the leathery faced foulmouthed old beardy bit player said about him. On the other hand, he wants to keep the men that 'sit on his right hand' happy. So, who amongst the Presidents entourage and close confidantes has an axe to grind with Mr. De Niro?

It's obvious!

The President's lawyer Rudy Giuliani of course!

But why? (I hear you ask).

The Godfather Part 11 – Best actor: Al Pacino, <u>Best supporting actor: Robert De Niro</u>.

Giuliani acted his socks off as the consigliore in that movie but never even got a mention. How deep the pools of hate and resentment run for those afflicted with the green eye of envy.

All I'll say is this.

Mr. Giuliani, stop dripping your poison into Donald Trump's ear and let it go. It was in 1974, for Chrissakes! Move on, man! Get a life.

Giuliani's time may yet come. I hear on the grapevine that alleged rapist Harvey Weinstein (no relation) may be looking for a bit player for his part in his up-coming rom-com romp, 'Me Too.' Giuliani should put himself forward for this, if he thinks his lawyering job isn't going that well. (He seems to be getting it wrong a lot lately). Poor old Harv can't leave his house and get to the studio with that bracelet on his leg. Giuliani looks a bit like him (bloated, sinister, pervy). If he went for the audition you'd be a 'shoe in.'

** The word 'smart,' was used by Mr. Trump to describe Chinaman Kim Jong Un at their recent carousal in Singapore. This is another of those words that has many dictionary definitions, and can be used as an adjective (clean, tidy, well dressed), a noun (intelligence, acumen), and a verb (a sharp stinging pain). I know which one I would apply as a description of both these 'great' men.

That's it for now.

Cheerio!

TRUMP / PUTIN NUCLEAR SUMMIT ON THE CARDS FOR LLANABER

There is a person currently olding high office that has self-delusions of such titanic proportion it is a potential threat to world peace. I do not refer in this case to the boss of America, Donald Trump. This is despite his declaration following the briefest of unstructured conflabs with the fat guy who's the boss of North Korea, Chinaman Kim, that there was now no longer a nuclear risk from that country.

His subsequent triumphantly bragnificent tweet read, and I quote verbatim:

"There is no longer a Nuclear Threat from North Korea. Everybody can now feel safer than the day I took office." How true this is.

The difference between the former President Barack Obama and the incumbent, Donald Trump, goes beyond intellect and temperament. The two men are like chalk (no offense intended) and cheese.

Obama would never dream of pressing the big red button without going through the pro's and con's then analyzing all the consequences. Then, and only then, would he commit the US to a retaliatory nuclear response, and only as a last resort after all other conciliatory avenues have been exhausted.

On the other hand, Trump, a thin skinned narcissist, would launch a nuclear attack on anybody that even so much as hinted that his gastric-banded wife was looking like she'd 'put on a bit of holiday weight.'

So, which one makes you feel safer, Obama the intellectual or Trump the nut job? (Where have I heard that phrase before).

Obviously the latter.

Why? Think back to your school days and all will become clear.

Say, for example, there are two boys in your class. Both are the same build but one is a bookworm and the other is a red neck on a hair trigger. It's your turn to buy the class' bagful of recreational drugs. Who do you take with you to do the trade with the bad boys on the corner, 'Speccy-Brainbox' or 'Mungo the meat-hammer?' Which do you think would make you feel safer having alongside you when money changed hands? I rest my case.

I digress. I was talking about a self-delusionary person in high office. I refer, of course, to none other than Mrs. Dorothy 'Binky' Trim, the boss of the parish council here in Llanaber. She is still fuming after being made to look a chump by Donald Trump in his double-shuffle regarding the renting of the room above her shop for his tryst with Chinaman Kim. She has a long memory and bears grudges.

Revenge is a dish best enjoyed cold and revenge was very much on the menu during the parish council meeting last night. This is where the self-delusionary element comes into my story. Mrs. T genuinely believes she can 'put one over' on Donald Trump. She has every intention of working a reverse double-flanker on the boss of America, and has even worked out a plan. Unfortunately, it is a plan that puts me at the center of a little vignette that could trigger world war three.

Let me 'fill you in.'

Mrs. T has caught on that Mr. Trump may be a little on the vain side. The blonde comb-over and brainiac is crowing from the rooftops about how smart he is for ridding the Korean peninsula from the threat of nuclear weapons before any have actually been removed, and without realizing this also includes the US nuclear threat to North Korea. In effect Trump has agreed with Kim Jong Un to rid the US of nukes.

As such, Mrs. T believes that if Trump is so dumb he can't see what he's done and so vain he needs something to crow about every now and then, she can easily fool him into trying to pull off the same trick with Vladimir Putin.

To this end she has instructed me, as parish Foreign Secretary, to write fraudulent letters to both Trump and Putin separately. I am to tell each that the other is seeking a discussion in a bid to secure bi-lateral nuclear disarmament between Russia and the US. Each will no longer be a nuclear threat to the other, and both men will emerge from the meeting as mega-heroes in the eyes of the world.

Which of these two humble peace-seekers could refuse this win-win offer?

I have been tasked to draft out two letters, one pretending to be Trump, and the other Putin. I must have both letters on her desk for her approval before close of business tonight, then have them in the post first thing tomorrow morning.

This is not a task in which I would wish to be complicit. If the ruse works and these two Ego-mountains meet, fine. But what if they start spitting at each other? Who knows what the consequences might be. Nevertheless it has fallen to me to do this and I'm nothing if not professional.

So, here goes:

"President Donald Trump
Boss of America

Dear President Putin,
May I call you Putty? You've no doubt seen how smart I am (on the TV etc. - assuming your backward little country has TV by now). I'm talking here about me and that fat kid from North Korea, Kim something or other. I got rid of all his bombs including the nukes just by letting him appear to be a pal of mine. He's a big headed chap (literally) therefore easily manipulated by a great guy and brainiac like me.
I want to do the same with you, Putty.
How about we meet? Let's say, in the room for rent above Mrs. Trim's sweet shop in the high street in Llanaber, next Tuesday at 2pm.
Mrs. Trim is a wonderful cook and I'm sure if I ask nicely she'll bake a batch of her magnificent commemorative airy-fairy cakes especially for the occasion. They're also a terrific value at $100 each.
So, is it a date, Putty?
Yes, of course it is!
See you there (perpetual fog permitting)

Donald

P.S. Don't bring the wife* and we can pull some of the local maidens and paint Llanaber red, eh?"
*(Pardon my clumsiness – are you married? I always suspected you had a bent towards the DUB side of the sexual spectrum, all that bare-chestedness and bear wrestling etc.)."

Letter no. 2

"President Vladimir (Vlad the Lad) Putin
    Boss of Russia (and anywhere else I take
    a fancy to)

Dear President Trump,
May I call you (let me refer to my notes here, Donald John Trump, the 45th and current President of the United States, in office only since January 20th, 2017)… New boy!
We're two fantastically great alpha-males, aren't we? You've got big hands, I've got big hands. How about we shake them eh, blondie? Let's say we meet and 'talk the big talk'- and I'm not talking the size of our dicks here, I'm talking NUKES!
Let's knock heads together in the room for rent in that beautiful Babushka Mrs. Trim's little sweet shop in the high street in Llanaber. I'm free next Tuesday at 2pm. How about you?
You know you want to. So I'll see you there, you big old Silverback!
I'm already looking forward to stripping off, oiling up and rolling on the floor with you in a grapple.
До скорой встречи. (see you later)

Vlad
P.S. How's about bringing some hot US crumpets for afters? The Russian ones are so cold."

I think I may be able to fool Mrs. T with this drivel but I'm not sure about Putin. As for Trump, I can already hear the check for the £25 room deposit winging its way to Llanaber as I write.
That's it for now.
Cheerio!

TRUMP CHARITY FUNDS SPENT ON HIS PORTRAIT – LLANABER BOSS WANTS IN

Part of my job as vilage Foreign Secretary requires me to be 'on the ball' when it comes to the gathering, analysis, and dissemination of world news, then to publish selected highlights in the Llanaber village newsletter. I have taken it upon myself to also act as a 'censor.' As such it is vital that I get to the village ticker tape early enough every morning to see the news tapes ahead of the boss of the parish council, Mrs. Dorothy 'Binky' Trim.

Why? (I hear you ask).
Obviously to destroy any news stories coming through on the ticker tape that may have a negative impact on Mrs. Trim's behavior.

Note – The ticker tape is the most reliable source of news in the village. Due to the perpetual fog, the TV signal in the village is atrocious. So, it's unlikely Mrs. T will pick up 'bad' stories from the television.

My track record to date in successfully 'vetting' the news has been 100%. However, today I failed in my duty. I stayed up too late last night in the hope that the perpetual fog would lift and I could watch a World Cup soccer match broadcast from Russia. No such luck. The picture was so distorted it would have been more entertaining looking out my window at the fog.

The upshot was that I slept in.

When I arrived at the ticker tape room in the council chambers this morning, Mrs. T was already there. She was holding a length of tape in her hand and grinning at me like Wanka Trump within half a mile of a camera. With a crazed look in her eye, she barked, "My office. NOW!"

There she showed me the news feed she had found. It read as follows:

"The attorney general of New York State sued the Donald J Trump charitable foundation, President Trump and three of his children on Thursday for violating state charity laws, alleging that the Trumps used charitable assets as 'little more than a checkbook for payments to not-for-profits from Mr. Trump and his companies.' The article went on to say:

"These include a $100,000 payment to settle legal claims against Mr. Trump's Mar-a-Lago resort, $158,000 to settle legal claims against Trump National Golf Club, and $10,000 to purchase a painting of Mr. Trump displayed at the Trump National Doral."

My heart sank when I was shown the story. I knew what would happen next.

Mrs. T, ever the one to jump on any Trump bandwagon or nick one of his bright ideas, immediately demanded that a portrait of our esteemed council leader (i.e. Mrs. T) be commissioned.

Also, her private lawyer and village pervert, Solly Weinstein (no relation) should have the legal bill for his defense settled straight away. I have no idea why. When Solly was recently prosecuted for harassing the village maidens into letting him measure their belly buttons he defended himself. I suspect the £100 fee she is demanding for Solly will pass straight through to Mrs. T herself (a sort of reverse Trump / Cohen pay off for his 'little thing' with Stormy Daniels).

I tried to point out that President Trump's ruse to use funds people had generously donated to his charity for his own selfish purposes had not worked. The President is being sued for $2.8 million in restitution and penalties. There then followed a long period of sustained crazy laughter from Mrs. T. When she calmed down, she said, "Do you really think that greedy man will ever pay them a cent?"

She had me there.

I naively asked her where the money was going to come from for her portrait. With an evil glint in her eye she said, "Scabby donkeys."

For those unfamiliar with Llanaber, there is a donkey concession on the beach. For the fee of £2 'Dai the Donkey' will let a punter sit on the back of one of his bandy legged nags for five minutes while their loved ones take snapshots through the swirling fog. It's a thriving business and Dai does okay.

But enough is never enough to these business mogul types. To supplement the fortune he earns from the donkey concession Dai runs a charitable organization called the 'Broke-Back Donkey Sanctuary.' To obtain funding for this mythical donkey paradise Dai has a life-sized plaster model of a knackered Mule with a slot in its head for punters to drop coins into. Gullible tourists look at the dreadful state of the actual bow-legged beasts he uses for the rides, burst into tears, then shove coins in the plaster coin-box like crazy. Dai empties it at the end of each shift then runs straight to the bank laughing.

Mrs. T has set her greedy eye on this fund. As the boss of the parish council she controls who does and who does not get a license to run the donkey concession on the beach. She has poor old Dai over a barrel.

It gets worse. There is only one painter in the village capable of completing a portrait with the final outcome being something that doesn't resemble swirling fog. That artist is called 'Screaming' Brenda Munch, a mad old bat that lives in the church bell tower. She's half blind and as deaf as a post. However, she is no slouch when it comes to a commission. The arthritic old bag is a very slow painter and charges by the hour. She'll have cleaned out Dai's 'scabby donkey' fund before the undercoat has dried on the canvas.

I have been given the tasks of a) giving Dai a 'quiet tap on the shoulder' about the con-box, and b) giving the good news to 'Screaming' Brenda about Mrs. T's portrait commission. I relish neither of these tasks.

But Mrs. T hadn't finished with me yet. With an even more evil glint in here eye she showed me the last section of the ticker tape concerning the lawsuit against the Trump family. I reproduce it for you here in full:

"The (Trump) foundation is little more than an empty shell that functions with no oversight from its board of directors. Trump ran the foundation according to whim, rather than law."

With an insane twisted grin, Mrs. T turned to me and said, "What do you think of the name, 'The Trim Foundation'?" Troubled times ahead, I fear.

I left her office and went straight out and bought a new alarm clock.

That's it for now.
Cheerio!

MOVES TO SENSOR "TRUMP WISDOM" FAIL IN LLANABER

I was up before the cock crow this morning to get to the news ticker tape ahead of the boss of the Llanaber village council, Mrs. Dorothy 'Binky' Trim. It's a good job I did. There were lots of small snippets that came through from the US about Trump that would have spelt trouble for the village if my esteemed leader got to see them. She is going through a phase of bandwagon jumping when it comes to the half-baked drivel that spurts from the cheese-ball headed comb-over's mouth. Below are a few of the craziest (and therefore most dangerous) Trump articles that I managed to censor:

a) Trump commenting on 'little rocket man' Chinaman Kim Jong Un:

"He speaks and his people sit up in attention. I want my people to do the same."

Mr. Trump is known across the globe as a garrulous slow-drawling idiot. If America suddenly went collectively insane enough to allow Trump to have his way on this, it would spell the end of slouching as we know it. Americans are famous for their slouching. They invented it and it looks cool. If you included mumbling in his troubled sleep, the amber faced anorexia denier Trump never shuts up. Americans would wake up, go through their day, then go to bed sitting up while the boring old nut job (where have I heard that phrase before) slowly burbles on, and on, and on ad infinitum.

That would be horror enough over in America, but what if Mrs. T imposed this as a new 'modus vivendi' in the council meetings?

Let me paint the picture.

Mrs. T has an unusual way of talking. She does not converse, as is traditional, to communicate, i.e. I say something then stop while you say something. Instead she talks in 'proclamations,' i.e. short staccato outbursts after which she has to take a long, wheezy, deep breath to recover – a bit like verbal projectile vomiting. There could be up to five minutes between each of Mrs. T's voluminous assertions. Therefore, at council meetings, we would be jerking up and down between slouching and sitting upright. Some of the councilors are getting annoyed. This could mess up their backs.

b) Trump reportedly praised North Korean state-run media and argued it was more favorable in its coverage than Fox News.

I too have noticed how positive the state run media is towards Chinaman Kim. Could it be that anyone who was 'less positive' towards Kim, would find themselves, along with their family and friends, on a fact finding tour of the nearest death camp within seconds of opening their dumb face-cave? The key words here, Mr. Trump, are 'state' and 'run.' So why should this article bother me? (I hear you cry).

Mrs. T has always wanted control of the village newsletter. If she thinks a precedent has been set in North Korea, she will make a power grab. Before you know it the newsletter will transmogrify from an informative news document into i) A polemic rant-rag against poor Mrs. Clinton, the old girl that runs the card shop, ii) a butt-licker eulogizing the achievements (Ha-ha!) of Mrs. Trim herself as our magnificent council leader and iii) an advert for Mrs. T's sweet shop, with a price list on the back.

c)   Trump's claim that his fine, upright, overly height-endowed exFBI boss, James Comey, committed 'criminal acts.'

From what I could glean from the ticker tape, Mr. Trump is yelling in everyone's ear that the ex-top-cop should be 'sent to prison' for deliberately doing his job.

Why is this bad news for Llanaber? (I hear you ask).

All I'll say is that if Trump gets his way over there then I fear for the future of our village top-cop Robert 'Robbie the Bobbie' Muller. Robbie has not yet published his report into the allegations of voting 'irregularities' that may have occurred during the 2016 election for Council leader. It's common knowledge throughout the village that the election was won over by 'the beast from the east' Putin Lotzadosh. Bribes were offered (free goes on the penny falls slot machines in Putin's arcade on the seafront). Bribes were accepted. But to date there is insufficient concrete and irrefutable evidence to prove that electoral fiddling took place.

Mrs. T is desperate to suppress Robbie's report and has tried everything within her powers to prevent its publication. This even includes sending Robbie the Bobbie and his entire extended family on a fact finding tour of bars and restaurants in the Florida Keys to 'study the effects of fast food and alcohol poisoning on sunbathers.'

Despite the fact that Robbie actually accepted this blatant bung, I still believe him to be an honest and upright law enforcer. Robbie speaks truth to power. The poor man's as dumb as a brick (where have I heard that phrase before?) He's so dumb he can't foresee the consequences when he opens his big stupid mouth. Therefore, I'm absolutely convinced he will publish his report in its entirety, warts and all, showing neither fear nor favor. This I expect he will do on his return sometime next year* from his fully expensed junket in Florida. (*or the year after, depending on how much Mrs. T can plunder from the village hospital's budget).

Despite my best efforts I was not able to stop one article from the ticker tape US news feed reaching Mrs. T. This one referred to Donald Trump unilaterally imposing a 25% tariff on selected goods imported from China. Both feet leapt straight onto the bandwagon, and I've been given strict instructions from Mrs. T to immediately impose a 1,000% tariff on all imported greetings cards bought in for resale in Llanaber. The average greetings card price has rocketed in the village as is now beyond the means of all but the deep pocketed American tourists (they are big spenders – their economy is booming). This is another blow aimed at poor old Mrs. Clinton who owns the card shop in the village and stood against her for council leader in 2016. As I've said in the past, Mrs. T has a long memory and bears grudges.

That's it for now.

Cheerio!

MAXIM'S 'MALE HOTTIES' LIST - LLANABER'S TOP 5 SUGGESTIONS

As a balanced, fair minded liberal white male in my sixties I was delighted when I read Maxim's annual hot 100 list to see that President Donald Trump's gastric banded 'lingerie model potential' wife, Melanie, and his thin grinning daughter, Wanka, have made the cut.

As a life-long campaigner against bigoted misogyny it's good to know that, in these unsettling ever changing times, the leftie, pinko, people pleasing, commie bed-wetters have at last won the day.

It's official! Women can now be classified as both 'hotties' and 'brainiacs.' Progress at last.

I take my hat off to you, Maxim's, for producing this bastion of modern thinking, although I must say I was surprised to see Prince Harry's new Misses, Angela Merkel, had made the grade. She's on the tubby side and looks a bit like a bloke. Then, I suppose it can't be easy to be the boss of Germany and a British royal at the same time. Too many free dinners, I suppose. She's bound to pile on the weight.

In these ground-breaking times in which we live, there have been many tireless warriors in the crusade to gain parity for women in society. In the vanguard of these great men is of course the champion for the de-objectification of women, Harvey Weinstein. His tireless efforts to bludgeon Joe public into seeing the half-clad, young, slender, beautiful women with their breasts half out their frocks that he parades in front of cameras as more than just sex objects is legendary.

That said, the forceps-birth-faced ex-movie mogul's effort to categorize the females he comes across (no pun intended) into two distinct camps, those worth raping and the rest (allegedly), was a complete disaster.

Why?

He failed to acknowledge that females can sometimes be clever. I'm of course referring here to the 'once-you've-made-me-rich-and-famous-I'll-rat-you-out-to-the-cops' ladies. I think they refer to themselves as the 'Me Too' victims for short.

Women? Clever? (I hear you ask).

Yes, it's not absurd, it is possible, and, believe it or not, quite common. Also, it occurs at the highest levels in society. This can be evidenced by anyone taking the trouble to look at what happened in the US election of 2016. One of the candidates was, in fact, a female. Further, she could have won the damned thing had the opposing candidate not had the sense to accept the kind offer of help from… let's just say a 'well-wisher.'

Yes, dear reader, women can be not only hot but brainy. Further, while being both eye-candy and smart they are also capable of popping out the occasional child. There's little doubt about it, women have a lot to offer modern society.

But there is still much work to do before women are fully considered equals to men.

So, it is right and proper in this forward thinking society of ours that women start to reciprocate in the objectification

stakes. To this end, I look forward to Maxim publishing their list of the top 100 male 'Red Hot
Brainiacs.'

Let me give Maxim a head start. Here's my pick in descending order:

At no. 5: Rudy Giuliani

Alright his brain is going a little soft these days, but he's still a magnificent example of the male physique after it has consumed far too many free meals at the taxpayer's expense. And those glasses are cool. Also, he wasn't bad as the consigliore in the Godfather, despite not getting nominated for an Oscar. Come on girls, give him another sideways glance!

At no. 4: Harvey Weinstein

The shy and self-deprecating 'Queen-maker' is nothing if not 'red hot.' Imagine seeing that man-beast completely naked (except for the ankle bracelet). Imagine that human tallow-barrel belly-flopping on top of you when he's off his medication and having one of his 'hot flushes' eh girls? Plus, every 'podge-pummeling' these days comes with the offer of a bit part in his upcoming rom-com romp, 'Me Too!' Need I say more!

At no. 3: Jared Kushner

He is a 'must-have' for women that like the weedy reptilian look in a man. I know he's someone most women would rather mother (or should that be smother?), but he has to be a veritable love machine in the sack. After all, you never see his thin, pasty-faced wife without a satisfied grin on her face.
Also, I think he has big hands. That's important to some women.

At no. 2: Vladimir Putin

Yes, the 'bear with no hair' himself. If you can overcome the homoerotic images of him half naked and wrestling bears, he comes across as quite a masculine man. How would you like to be 'annexed' by him, eh ladies? How do you fancy one of his surface-to-surface missiles heading towards your strategic regions? Sure, you might struggle with snogging those wafer thin lips, but wouldn't you just die for having the 'Baldy Bolshevik' smearing his unidentified substances on your front door, know what I mean girls?

At no. 1: Donald Trump

Need I say more, the ultimate alpha-male! What a magnificent example of the perfect physique for a fat bloke. Even his eyelids boast several layers of podge. For all those female 'feeders' out there he's a 'must have.' You only have to look at the quality of the totty he surrounds himself with to see that the man is beyond question a human fanny magnet. If you think he's a hunk fully clothed standing at the lectern telling everyone how smart he is, then just imagine him stripped naked, lying on his stomach, his head tilted coquettishly towards the camera above and to his right.

Can you imagine that, ladies?

That 'all-over' tan, even in the folds of his man boobs. That blonde hair, luscious and long, cascading loosely and seductively from the sides of his head as he pouts at the lens. That bald patch glistening in the warm pink / blue glow from the sunbed lamps as he beckons you towards him with his stubby little index finger.

And girls, don't forget, beneath that disheveled comb-over lurks the biggest mega-brain in the whole goddamn world.

What a body!

What a brain!

And all in one person – the complete package. Mr. Sexy-Brainiac, dished up on a sun-bed platter, just for you!

Alas, dear ladies, it could never be. This is all just fantasy.

All these men are spoken for** and are in long term relationships, happily married, some with families. All are men of complete and utter probity and would not conscience a dalliance outside the bounds of wedlock. Mr. Trump has even spoken at length on the subject, both publicly and privately to his lawyer while handing over a bag containing $130,000 in grubby used notes (allegedly).

So, my advice to you, ladies, is to admire these magnificent creatures from afar. Certainly never get within groping distance of Pervy Weinstein unless you fancy a bit part in his upcoming rom-com romp, 'Me Too!'

** I'm not sure about Putin. I understand he's divorced but with all the topless man-grappling he does, he strikes me as a man with a leaning towards the 'DUB' sexual preference.

N.B. Mrs. Trim must never find out about the Maxim's list. She's still spitting blood about not being nominated for the Nobel Peace prize (yet). Not making the Maxim's top 100 might tip her over the edge.

That's it for now.

Cheerio!

RONNA MCDANIEL'S ATTEMPT TO 'CRUSH ALL DISSENT' IMPACTS LLANABER.

There is a new phrase on the lips of the old dingbat who is the boss of the parish council here, Mrs. Dorothy 'Binky' Trim. It is: "Complacency is our enemy. Anyone that does not embrace the Dorothy Trim agenda for making Llanaber great again will be making a big mistake."

This rather sinister locution suddenly appeared in a very threatening way in the middle of the parish council meeting last night. Let me fill you in on the background.

With her usual modesty and self-effacement, Mrs. Trim was treating us to another diatribe about what makes her tenure as parish leader better than that of anyone else in the entire history of time. Normally it's just a prolonged rant during which most of us wander off to the bathroom or make a cup of tea, her tortuous and convoluted reasoning being mostly rhetorical, and all over the place like a mad woman.

But last night was different. Midst the nonsensical talk Mrs. T started referring to her 'five point plan' to make, and I quote, "This poxy village of ours great again."

She then started handing out A4 photocopies of her master plan to bring prosperity back to the village. When I saw what was on the sheet, my heart sank. I reproduce for you below in its entirety. Mrs. Trim's five point plan is:

No. 1 - Big up the tourist attractions in the village by printing a brochure full of lies to draw in more punters.

No. 2 - Squeeze every cent possible out of the dolts that come by charging extortionate entrance fees to the attractions.

No. 3 - Build a castle with the profits.

No. 4 - Add the castle to the brochure. Re-print the pack of lies but now include the real castle. This will draw in even more mug punters.

No. 5 - Repeat steps 1 to 4.

After handing out the sheets, she sat back proudly in her chair and started slapping herself on her back in a congratulatory way.

The room fell silent.

"Questions?" she asked, giving all of us her 'anyone that pipes up will get crucified' look.

But surprisingly a lot of questions were asked. Below I briefly summarize the questions that were asked with the corresponding responses from Mrs. T:

Q: 'Apart from the fog bound beach, does the village actually have any attractions?'

A: 'Complacency is our enemy. Anyone that does not embrace the Dorothy Trim agenda for making Llanaber great again will be making a big mistake.'

Q: 'If we get more tourists what can we do to hide the ghastly sink hole full of garbage in the main street?'

A: 'Complacency is our enemy. Anyone that does not embrace the Dorothy Trim agenda for making Llanaber great again will be making a big mistake.'

Q: Is it morally acceptable to knowingly print and distribute a pack of lies in a brochure glorifying crappy attractions, some of which don't actually exist?'

A: 'Complacency is our enemy. Anyone that does not embrace the Dorothy Trim agenda for making Llanaber great again will be making a big mistake.'

Q: 'If we built this castle then who would live in it?'

A: 'ME!'

We all traipsed out of the council meeting with our eyes downcast, convinced that the old bag had finally gone 'skitzidoodle.' Where on earth had she got this 'complacency' nonsense from?

It was when I did my early morning stint in the news feed ticker tape room in the parish offices that the metaphorical fog lifted (N. B. outside the fog was still as thick as Donald Jr.). There was a piece about a sinister and intimidating tweet from Ronna McDaniel, the Chair of the Republican National Committee in the US, and niece of that shy and retiring liberal, Mitt Romney. McDaniels' threatening tweet was virtually word for word the phrase Mrs. T had used, and with the same objective, i.e. to crush all dissent.

Oh dear! Troubled times ahead here and in the US, I fear.

One genuinely positive act Mrs. T has performed this week is well worth a mention. The apparent triumph of infallible anorexia denier and suntan bed user Donald Trump's summit meeting with Chinaman Kim Jong Un inspired the old fruit-bat to summon the head of the Druids, Benjy Yahoo, to her office for a 'dressing down.'

This is unusual behavior for Mrs. T as she's as thick as thieves with the rich and powerful Druid tribe and wouldn't normally do anything that might 'tick them off.' But seeing the triumphant crowing by the Trump camp after their meeting, she sees an opportunity to step onto the global stage by playing the great peacemaker. Also, the Druids are getting a lot of bad press lately. They've started beating the Traveler's kids in public again and feeding the limbs that are left over to their devil dogs.

The fact that the Druids and the Travelers have been at each other's throats since time began didn't seem to put the old girl off.

Benjy was duly summoned.

My hopes were high for a positive outcome. Despite the fact that it is village council policy that we remain neutral in this long running dispute (but secretly side with the Druids), I feel sorry for the travelers. It can't be nice for them being imprisoned on that sand dune 24/7 with only one hose pipe and the occasional food parcel from Oxfam.

The Trim / Yahoo summit was very short.

I reproduce the minutes below:

"<u>Agenda</u>: To discuss the way forward to bring about a lasting peace between the Druids and the Travelers.

Present: Mrs. D 'Binky' Trim,

    Mr. B. Yahoo,

Mr. D. Smith (for the purpose of minute taking only)

Mrs. Trim opened the meeting by asking that, in the light of the recent successful summit between Donald Trump and Kim Jong Un, would Mr. Yahoo reconsider his position on the legitimacy of the Traveler's claims on the Arcade along the seafront in Druidellau.

There was a fifteen minute break taken, allowing time for Mr. Yahoo to stop laughing.

Once calm, Mr. Yahoo responded by telling Mrs. Trim to 'get stuffed.' The meeting was then adjourned with no set date to reconvene. Mrs. Trim and Mr. Yahoo then left for a round of golf in the fog and a slap up lunch at the Druid's expense." All credit to Mrs. T. She did try.

That's all for now.

Cheerio!

KELLY CRAFT DEATH THREAT POWDER COULD BE SKIN FLAKES

Source: https://globalnews.ca/news/3819311/kelly-knight-craft-us-ambassador-canada/

There was a report on the parish news feed ticker tape this morning that US Ambassador to Canada, Kelly Craft, has received death threats. It was reported that a package containing white powder and a threatening letter peppered with expletives was sent to the lady in question.

Pundits with their head stuck up their bottoms have put this down to the spitting contest currently taking place between the shy and retiring brainiac and anorexia denier, Donald Trump, and his opposite number up in Mounty-County, the effete Justin Trudeau.

I think these so-called news buffs have got it completely wrong.

It is obvious to me who is behind this nasty and cowardly little trick. Think, dear reader, outside the proverbial box full of white powder. Who would wish harm upon this harmless dishy diplomat?

Who indeed! There is a school of thought that the prank is nothing more than another of Donald's reverse back-shaftings. By this I mean the Duck himself, or one of his henchmen, sent the parcel.

But why? (I hear you ask).

Obviously, to encourage more patriotic rabid right wingers to get off their lazy butts and do something nasty to a Canadian in retaliation. It's a simple call to arms by the President

But who sent it? (I hear you ask again).

Perhaps some dumb as a brick (where have I heard that phrase before?) red neck Trump obsessive, like, for example, Steve Bannon?

Or perhaps one of Donald Trump's 'bagmen,' i.e. someone well practiced in doing the cheese-ball headed mega-brain's dirty work? Here I'm thinking of someone like Michael Cohen?

Or could it have been one of the big hitters who 'sit on Donald Trump's right hand?' Here I'm thinking of the 'loudmouthed fart' John Bolton and the 'Albino lizard' Mike Pence, or perhaps even Mr. Body-Beautiful himself, Jeff Sessions? (Please note I do not point the finger of blame at poor old addled brained Rudy Giuliani here. He's been getting it wrong a lot lately. If it had been him, he would probably have sent the parcel to Stormy Daniels by mistake; and have written his name and address on the back).

Then there is the possibility that Kelly Craft posted the thing to herself.

Why not? It's plausible.

The woman could be an insecure attention seeker, or a fanatic career diplomat, a rare breed, desperate to climb to the top of the greasy diplomatic pole. The sympathy generated towards her following a death threat would give her career a nice little boost. She is already the Canadian ambassador for the US. Could there be a higher post on the diplomatic hierarchical ladder than Canada?

Yes, of course there is.

Antigua and Barbuda!

Why? Canada's a rotten posting. It's a freezing cold shit-hole, culture desert and full of towns where there's only one surname. Antigua and Barbuda by contrast has cheap booze, sandy beaches, carnivals every other day, hunky men and best of all, great weather (bar the hurricanes), and all of this with the added bonus of not having an over-bloated, over-sexed, ham fisted ego-monster of a boss slobbering all over you. Trump would never dream of attending summits in 'shit-hole countries' like these.

But I for one do not for one second believe any of the above theories. Which brings me to my point, i.e. who really did send the nasty parcel?

There is no doubt about it in my mind the 'box of bile' was sent by none other than Melanie Trump!

There, it's out.

Once the forensic genii (or is it geniuses?) have completed their analysis, they will undoubtedly discover that the white powder is nothing more than dead skin flakes. I refer here to the natural exfoliation that constantly flutters from the face of the President's gastric banded and 'lingerie model potential' wife.

Let me paint the scenario for you.

Melanie is at home sitting on the settee under a blanket, recovering from her gastric band operation and getting beaten by her chubby-hubby after she queries why she was mysteriously $130,000 down in her housekeeping. She then idly switches on the TV and channel hops while reading about herself in Maxim's top 100 'list of hotties.' The channel alights on the arrival of her husband at the G7 meeting. The news article catches her attention and, with a super-human effort, she manages momentarily to tear her eyes away from admiring her pictures in the shag-rag to watch the news article. There she sees her cuddly butterball of a husband stumble down the steps of the posh US tax payer funded plane straight into the arms of another woman! In an instant she is beside herself with jealousy and rage.

There, in front of the world's media, she suffers the penultimate humiliation - her husband caressing another brainy-babe in public! (N.B. The ultimate humiliation is, of course, having your husband pay off a porn queen $130,000 to keep her mouth, if not her legs, shut).

Melanie is incandescent. She must have her revenge! She drags her skinny carcass off her sick bed and stumbles to her posh bureau and there she scribbles the 'string of vile consciousness' letter to her nemesis Kelly Craft. Her head is shaking with rage as each repugnant word scratched out is torn from her soul. Hence, dear reader, the copious amounts of white powder.

For now I rest my case. In time the truth will 'out' and my theory of who is the perpetrator of this outrage against Kelly Craft will be proven correct.

But what about justice? (I hear you ask yet again).

Melanie Trump is a powerful lady, true, but no one, not even her, should be above the law. Appropriate punishment should be meted out justly and proportionately, no matter what ones position in the societal hierarchy. Even the most powerful must bend their knee to the overarching might of the laws of the land.

I am a great believer that the punishment should fit the crime. In this case, I believe it would be highly appropriate for Kelly Craft to write down a few nasty comments about Melanie's robot face on a sheet of A4 paper, liberally sprinkle the letter with expletives and put it in a cardboard box. Then Ms. (or is it Mrs.?) Craft should fill the remaining space in the box with dandruff and fluff from her navel, and then post the vile bloody thing to Melanie.

Let me add one more comment about crime and punishment.

I genuinely believe that making the punishment fit the crime would have been adopted as the most appropriate system of administering justice throughout the world had it not been for one unsolvable problem.

How do you punish a flasher?

That's it for now.

Cheerio!

AG SESSIONS' BIBLE QUOTE RAISES DIFFICULT QUESTIONS FOR TRUMP

United States Attorney General Jeff Sessions delivers remarks during the 30th Annual Candlelight Vigil to memorialize fallen officers on the National Mall in Washington, D.C., May 13, 2018. U.S. Customs and Border Protection Photo by Glenn Fawcett

I believe in a God of some sorts, even though his existence defies modern science and logical thinking. So it was comforting to hear the quietly mad US Attorney General and Adonis, Jeff Sessions, quoting the bible in a political context.

Why? (I hear you ask).

In order to justify the US administration's current policy of dragging the children of undocumented illegal immigrants kicking and screaming from their helpless parents' arms should they get caught.

I quote the snowy white headed lunatic below verbatim:

"I would cite you to the Apostle Paul and his clear and wise command in Romans 13, to obey the laws of the government because God has ordained the government for his purposes // Our policy that can result in short-term separation of families is not unusual or unjustified."

It's not often I can say that pearls of wisdom have dripped from this old duffer's drawling gob, but in this case I wholeheartedly agree (about the God thing, not the moronic separation of kids from their parents). The snowy-topped 'sideways glancer' Sessions seems to be suggesting a pre-ordained modus vivendi straight from the almighty of 'do as we (the administration) say, for we are the Government and therefore God's earthly instruments and beyond reproach.'

I couldn't agree more. It cuts out all this wasted effort by those with a different point of view (i.e. the pesky wet, liberal, left wing, commie, people pleasing, troublemakers and naysayers) and their incessant peeping into dark corners to scrutinize what this administration gets up to.

In fact, the bible thumping AG should have gone further. By this I mean by quoting further from Romans 13, not killing the kids in front of their parents for good measure.

For example: Romans Chapter 13, verse 1:

"Let everyone be subject to the governing authorities, for there is no authority except that which God has established. The authorities that exist have been established by God."

But hold on! Wouldn't this, if followed to the letter, create a problem for the President?

Surely there are governments around the world, also by definition put there by God that the American administration isn't exactly a big fan of? For example, Iran, Syria, Yemen, Lebanon, Pakistan, Palestine territories, Tunisia, Slovenia, Sudan, Russia & Soviet aligned countries, Cuba, Venezuela, China and until recently North Korea to name but a few.

So, if God put these governments into power, it must follow that any aggressive act towards these countries by the current administration is going against the will of God.

If AG Sessions had quoted from another later verse he would have created yet another moral dilemma, especially for Mr. Trump himself:

Romans, chapter 13, verse 6:

"This is also why you pay taxes, for the authorities are God's servants, who give their full time to governing. 7Give to everyone what you owe them: If you owe taxes, pay taxes;"

No doubt, the righteous Mr. Sessions, even as I write, is pressing his slippery, tax law savvy boss, Donald Trump, into publishing his long awaited non-redacted tax returns. Then we can all be reassured the Duck is compliant with God's will, and coughing up every cent he owes the US government for his obscene earnings from his vast business empire.

It might also have been embarrassing if the old fart had quoted Romans, chapter 13, verse 13 were it not for his boss' complete and utter probity:

Let us behave decently, as in the daytime, not in carousing and drunkenness, not in sexual immorality and debauchery, not in dissension and jealousy."

It is a matter of record that Donald Trump does not drink, but I know there are some amongst us that are not sure about the rest.

Is he sexually immoral or a debaucher?

I for one am convinced that he is not; otherwise God would never have made him the boss of America. It therefore follows that he could <u>never</u> have laid so much as a stray lip on the shy, demure Stormy Daniels. He could have saved himself the 130,000 smackers he bunged her to keep her face-hole shut if he'd just have trusted in the Lord.

Is he prone to dissension and jealousy?

Obviously not. The constant barrage of positivity that comes from his tweets, frequently praising those that may not see eye to eye with him, stands as testimony to that.

All I can say is 'well done God' for getting it right and putting Donald Trump into office as the President of the United States.

That said, if or when Robert Mueller publishes the results of his enquiries, it transpires it wasn't so much the hand of God as the interfering hands of a certain bald headed Russian that influenced the election in 2016. If it was Putin that helped squeeze the Duck into office, then what bible quoting spin will Mr. Sessions put on that?

It must be a worrying time for Mr. Trump having that report hanging over him like the sword of Damocles. If I can offer you my humble advice, Mr. President? Don't worry. Take heart, stay cool, hold your nerve and start praying.

Heed ye the words of Philippians, chapter 4, verse 6:

"Do not be anxious about anything, but in everything, by prayer and petition, with thanksgiving, present your requests to God."

You never know your luck. He just might hear your prayers and, through his omnipotence, empower 'Vlad the bad' to swing into action again and get one of his henchmen to smear 'an unknown substance' on Mr. Mueller's front door before the report gets published.

From my part I know that I will be facing another sleepless night tonight. If the words of the religious nut job (where have I heard that phrase before?) Sessions ever reach the ears of my esteemed leader, Mrs. Dorothy 'Binky' Trim, then the village is in for a shaky future.

It's bad enough that she is so self-deluded that she believes she won the 2016 Llanaber council leader election fair and square. It's common knowledge that 'the beast from the east' Putin Lotzadosh influenced the result by bribing voters with free goes on the penny falls machines in his arcade. If she finds out it was God himself that put her into power, and what's more, to challenge anything she does is going against God's will, then I fear for the pittance still remaining in the village hospital's budget. Also, I wouldn't hold out much hope for the long term prospects of her defeated opponent, old Mrs.

Clinton who runs the village card shop.
As I've said before, Mrs. T has a long memory and bears grudges.
That's it for now.
Cheerio!

'TRUMP TO SEND ILLEGALS' KIDS INTO SPACE' RUMOR
REACHES LLANABER

As Robert Burns once so famously said, 'The best laid schemes o' mice an' men gang aft a-gley.' If you need it gtranslated, it means you might have a great plan but it can still get bolloxed. It was thus so yesterday. My assiduous efforts to deny the boss of the parish council, Mrs. Dorothy 'Binky' Trim access to the news feed ticker tape in the parish council building have been near perfect. I've been up early and have successfully filtered out any story that might influence the old bag that may result in a negative impact on village life. Also, I've been very lucky with the weather. Perpetual fog has lain heavy on the village for the last ten days. Whilst this hammers the tourist trade (the fog is especially thick in summer and we lose the occasional visitor into the massive sink hole in the high street) it has meant that there has been no TV signal, so Mrs. T has not been able to pick up news from that source.

Why am I so eager to deny my esteemed leader access to up to the minute world news? (I hear you ask).

Mrs. T is becoming increasingly obsessed with mirroring any crazy idea coming from the United States in general and from Donald Trump in particular. She has become a bandwagon jumper of mammoth proportions (literally – she's worked in her sweet shop since she was a toddler, so she 'doesn't need much water in the bath' if you get my drift).

So, why the reference to Robert Burns? (I hear you ask again).

I have erred!

I failed to take into consideration the news source used most frequently in Llanaber. I refer here to the official village gossip, Mrs. Winfrey, who, by the way, has aspirations of standing against Mrs. T for the job of boss of the council in the next election. She doesn't stand a snowball in Hell's chance. She blabs continuously, and can't be trusted with a secret. It's imperative that the village boss can keep his or her face shut; otherwise everyone will know what's happening to the village hospital's budget.

I digress. I was bringing you up to speed with the latest development in the village.

Mrs. T, as you may recall, runs the sweet shop in the village, 'Nanny Trim's Sweets 'N' Stuff.' Mrs. Winfrey is partial to fudge. She would normally score her supply from old Mrs. Clinton who runs the card shop, but the poor old girl is still locked up in prison after Mrs. T flushed her out as being a rabid commie subversive, in an Arkady Babchenco style sting.

The upshot was that Mrs. Winfrey had to buy her fudge from Mrs. T's shop, which she was reported as saying was 'just as good.'

N. B. For the avoidance of doubt, Mrs. T's fudge is NOT 'just as good.' I know for a fact that Mrs. Clinton puts more butter in her recipe.

All went swimmingly with the transaction until Mrs. Winfrey started to offload her gossip. That's when the damage was done. As soon as Mrs. Winfrey had waddled out of the shop (she eats a lot of fudge) Mrs. T closed up her shop and called an immediate extra-ordinary council meeting.

What did Mrs. Winfrey say that had so spooked Mrs. T? (I hear you ask yet again).

Before I answer my rhetorical question let me tell you a little about Mrs. Winfrey. She has a tendency to conflate her stories inasmuch as three separate stories go in her ears and one comes out of her mouth. With this made clear, this is what she said to Mrs. T. (verbatim):

"President Trump is separating children from the parents of illegal immigrants and making them join a new 'Space Force' to be used to reduce the outrageously increased levels of crime that now exists in Germany because of runaway illegal immigration."

She went on to add:

"It's an exquisite solution in that the President is using these illegal kids to dive in from their satellites in outer space to get rid of their illegal parents in a massive 'zero tolerance crime' clamp down."

Mrs. T didn't for one minute seem to think this was all jumbled up crazy nonsense. Quite the opposite. At the extraordinary council meeting she banged on the table, pointed an accusing finger at me, and shouted, "What the hell are you doing about this?"

I asked what she would like me to do. It was a mistake.

"Isn't it obvious?" she barked, glaring daggers at me, "Round up the undocumented illegal families in the village, drag the kids away from them, train them to be parenticidal astronauts, then fire them into space!"

I foolishly pointed out that there were several barriers to the successful completion of her instructions. These are but some:

a) The village has no undocumented illegal families. The best we can boast is the occasional visit by a bunch of 'rowdies' from the failing neighboring village, Spanibont. Even their visits have declined since Mrs. T appointed one of the rowdies, 'Mateo the Knife,' as the head of village homeland security.

b) Llanaber doesn't have a space program, let alone a space ship
capable of firing even a single child into the upper atmosphere.

c) Even if we were able to 'rent' a space ship we wouldn't know what to do with it. For your information: While it has never been confirmed as fact, it is rumored that there are at least two people in the area with fully functioning rockets. It's strongly suspected that the leader of the Druids, Benjy Yahoo, owns a secret stock of 'rockets.' Our village cop, Robert 'Robbie the Bobbie' Muller once discovered a stash of them hidden in Benjy's garage. Benjy made up a story up to tell Robbie, telling him that they were for 'a special fireworks display' he was planning for the Travelers.

Also, the owner of the village amusement arcade, the 'beast from the east' Putin Lotzadosh recently 'annexed' the local swamp, Bogbourne, into his slot machine empire. He claimed this was for the storage of his perfectly harmless life sized model tanks, battleships, and rockets. I've seen them through my binoculars. I suspect some may not be models, in particular the ones with warheads.

d) It's traditional for kids to love their parents, not kill them.

Mrs. T would have none of it.

But for once I was thinking on my feet. I pointed out that while
America and Germany have problems with illegal human immigrants,
Llanaber has a huge problem with illegal sheep. Because there is not yet a fence between Llanaber and Spanibont (they still refuse to pay for it), the bloody things stray in from Spanibont and eat our grass.

Also, the village may not have a rocket but it does have an alternative. In the year 1766, Llanaber was engaged in a brief war with Spanibont over which village had the rights to the collection of excrement from the fields for fertilizing the leek plantations. We won because we had better weaponry, i.e. a large wooden catapult. The village still has this catapult, and it has been meticulously maintained. Not only is it in perfect working order, but it is capable of firing a four week old lamb for a distance of over ten yards.

It was just as I pointed this out that I played my trump card (no pun intended).

I produced a large bagful of Turkish Delight and put it on the table in front of Mrs. T. She cannot resist the stuff. She went into it straight away. She has the attention span of an amoeba, so within moments she'd waved me away to 'get on with it' while she stuffed her fat face with the remains of the sickly confection.

I left the council building and went straight to see Mrs. Winfrey. I gave her £1 to spend on fudge and told her the story about how Donald Trump had just resigned and left The White House to jog naked to the South Pole.

Let's hope Mrs. T jumps on that bandwagon.

That's it for now.

Cheerio!

LLANABER FOLLOWS US LEAD AND PULLS OUT OF HUMAN RIGHTS ORGANIZATION

Two pieces of bad news from the village to report today, both of which I'm convinced will spell long term problems for Llanaber.

Firstly, the boss of the village, Mrs. Dorothy 'Binky' Trim, has pulled Llanaber out of BUTT (Bandage Up the Toddlers).

BUTT is a county wide human rights organization set up to monitor injustices being perpetrated on the weaker tribes in the county. By 'shining a light' into the dark corners of mostly covert, but unfortunately frequently overt acts of barbarism performed on the helpless, the organization hopes to shame the perpetrators into behaving in a more civilized way. It's a noble endeavor, and all the villages in the county are active members.

Admittedly it has yet to have a single success.

Why? (I hear you ask).

Because it is an organization with no teeth (not literally – it includes a delegate from a village on the mountain, Blaenau Ffullinagob, where the villagers all have a mouthful of buck teeth). What I mean is that they can point at something bad that's happening, jump up and down, shout and scream about it until they're blue in the face, but ultimately the perpetrators can stick their fingers up at BUTT and carry on regardless. It's a 'name and shame' outfit, not one that has genuine power to act.

Also, the delegates are scared of making waves. They are all career councillors and would never support criticizing the boss of any of the villages. i.e. someone in a job more senior to theirs, in case 'the black spot' was put on their file.

Is being a member of BUTT arduous? (I hear you ask again). Is that why Mrs. T has pulled the village out of this 'do-gooder' organization?

I would say not.

Each village sends a single delegate to the monthly meeting in a café on the sea front here in the village. They enjoy a good lunch on expenses during which they ask each other if they've seen anything nasty going on 'here or hereabouts.' As the perpetual fog prevents anybody seeing anything, the answer from each delegate is usually in the negative. They all then have another pot of tea and a round of cakes, and then shuffle off back to their day jobs worrying about their cholesterol levels.

So the upshot is that BUTT exists in perpetual harmony with the county council regardless of whatever 'evil doings' are happening in the real world. By this I refer, obviously, to the Druids and their on-going persecution of the Travelers, where a 'blind eye' has to be turned by all the delegates at every meeting.

It is my responsibility to write and circulate the minutes. This usually takes the form of half a paragraph of the negative results scribbled on a sheet of A4 paper and circulated to all the county's 'village bosses.' Job done.

But not so at the last meeting. It was a complete nightmare.

Why? (you may ask).

Mrs. Winfrey!

She is the official village gossip, and just happened to be in the café on the next table enjoying a cup of coffee and a slice of Bara Brith (local bread made with sawdust). She was eavesdropping all the way through the BUTT meeting. When I went round the table asking each delegate the usual question she piped in.

"What about the Travelers' kids!" she blurted out.

Mrs. Winfrey can usually be relied on to conflate five or six stories into one and get it all wrong. But in this case she had been succinct, a single short sentence!

We had nowhere to run. She had us by the balls!

We could no longer turn a collective blind eye to the blatant cruelty meted out by the Druids on the Travelers' tribe. I had to come clean. I had myself only that morning passed through the next village along, Druidellau, and witnessed first-hand the Druidian 'devil dogs' being set upon a Traveler's child, a newspaper delivery boy, and tearing the backside out of the twelve year old's trousers. One of the dogs even cocked its leg on the poor lad's newspaper bag. I felt a wave of shame roll over my head. I couldn't look my fellow delegates in the eye. This travesty of justice and blatant persecution of the Travelers by the Druids must no longer be allowed. The county MUST be officially notified.

With downcast 'eyes of shame' I include the following in my BUTT monthly report:

"Please be aware that the Druids are terrible people and frequently kick around the totally innocent Travelers. Despite never being officially reported, it is common knowledge that the Druids' henchmen keep the Travelers cooped up on a single sand dune on the beach and only allow them one hose pipe for water. The Druids are a nasty bunch that block the golf course so no one else gets a look in, and their boss, Benjy Yahoo, is a big headed liar."

I felt better. I felt clean for the first time in a longtime. It was at last 'on the record.'

I felt good about myself.

However, Mrs. T did not feel good about me.

When she saw my report she went skitziloopy. She demanded that I retract my statement.

I stood firm.

Right is might!

I refused to buckle under the immense pressure of 'the establishment.' I felt I was on solid ground and would win the day.

As she looked at me, a twisted grin formed on her face. "Okay," said Mrs. T, "I'm pulling us out of BUTT."

I was gobsmacked. It was like a blow to my manly bits.

She went on, "BUTT is an organization not worthy of its name and a cesspool of political bias."

Where had this come from?

Then it hit me. I hadn't reckoned on the American factor.

While I was enjoying my slap up lunch with my buddies from BUTT in seafront café, Mrs. T had been in the council news feed ticker tape room. She must have been rifling through the waste bin and found the report I'd 'censored' earlier that day. It was the report that the US had just pulled out of the United Nations Human Rights Council. Nikki Haley had managed to stay out of the ladies' restroom long enough (I think she still has a touch of the 'titus' despite us sending her a crate of Cranberry juice from our overseas aid budget) to make a speech using the same phrase Mrs. T just had.

In Nikki Haley's case, she was throwing the American toys out of the pram over what she considered to be unfair criticism of the Israelis.

N.B. I can't believe so much fuss is being made over a few Palestinian troublemakers getting gunned down in cold blood by Israeli snipers with high power rifles. It was clear in the news footage these children were 'armed and dangerous' with their catapults.

"So, no more free lunches for you, Mr. Man of Principles," said Mrs. T as she bundled me out of her office.

She's right. Speaking truth to power has its consequences. In my case it's a free monthly steak & chips with all the trimmings, or now, the lack of it.

And what was the other piece of bad news? (I hear you ask).

Mrs. Trim has bought a cell phone, the first in the village. She plundered the village hospital budget and sent off for one. It arrived today.

"At last we can enjoy the benefits of social networking," she crowed excitedly as she showed the bloody thing off in the council meeting.

We?

She's the only one that has one, so who is she going to network with?

Nevertheless, I'm dreading the day the village gets cell phone signal. That's it for now.

Cheerio!

DEMOCRACY UNDER THREAT FROM BRUTAL ZERO TOLERANCE POLICY

Jennifer Loy @themyscira_blog

There is a new word that has suddenly appeared in the lexicon of the esteemed leader of Llanaber parish council, Mrs. Dorothy Binky' Trim. To be precise it is two words; 'Zero tolerance.'

I know from the news feeds coming through on the village ticker tape that this phrase will be filling with horror the hearts (if not the pants) of undocumented illegal immigrants sneaking around in the dark shadowy desert just the richer side of the Mexican / US border.

But why should the phrase bother me, or anyone else, here in Llanaber? (I hear you ask).

Let me fill you in. Recently Mrs. T's brain has been filled with a plethora of batty ideas all emanating from the masters

159

of batty ideas, Donald Trump's US administration. The most damaging of the nonsense wandering about in Mrs. T's empty brain are:

a) She believes that being the council leader is the 'will of God' and, as God's instrument on Earth, she must be obeyed without question. That's down to the selective bible quoting from the lunatic 'sideways-glancer' Jeff Sessions.

b) She also believes that she has the power to pardon herself should she ever do anything wrong. That one's down to the wild-eyed, bloated consigliore from the Godfather, Rudi Giuliani.

c) She believes that it is axiomatic that when she became the village top dog it was because God made it happen. As God is omnipotent, everything she does as 'His instrument' must be beyond question the right thing to do. I think the Duck himself is responsible for this one.

Therefore, in summary, because she believes that everything she says is true and everything she does is correct, it follows that every one of her orders must be obeyed to the letter without question or dissent.

The following story deals with the first part of the statement above, i.e. that everything Mrs. T says is true by edict.

At last night's council meeting an incident occurred that caused Mrs. T to eyeball us all menacingly and say, and I quote verbatim, "Matthew, chapter 12, verse 30, 'whoever is not with me is against me.'"

(I think I can jointly blame Ronna McDaniel's attempt to 'Crush All Dissent,' and the bible thumping sideways-glancer Sessions for this one).

But why did she suddenly do this? (I hear you cry).

Because there was dissent in the ranks!

Let me paint the picture for you.

The incident happened immediately following the short break we have at about 7.00pm for a cup of tea and a slice of Bara Brith, the confection made from bread ingredients and sawdust that is a favorite amongst the villagers. As time was pressing, Mrs. T told us to take our teas and snacks back into the council chambers so the meeting could continue.

This we did.

When we had all resumed our seats, Mrs. T took a quick slurp of her tea before calling the meeting to order. As she returned her cup to its saucer, she grimaced and said, "This coffee is cold."

The room immediately fell into a deafening silence. We all looked at each other. Who would be the one amongst us brave enough to correct Mrs. T's error? I decided it would be old councillor Thomas, the village grave digger (an honorary title – the village doesn't have a graveyard), and gently prodded him in his testicles under the table with my boot. He understood immediately what was required of him.

"Hahem," he coughed quietly, "Er… I think you'll find it's tea, your worshipfulness."

Mrs. T glared pure hate at the poor old duffer before, barely audibly, uttering the aforementioned bible quote.

It was then that I noticed something I'd never seen before. There was a small, silver bell to the right of the papers on the desk in front of Mrs. T. Still glaring at old Thomas, she lifted up the little bell and gave it a shake. It let out the quietest of tinkles, but the effect was monumental.

The doors to the council chamber crashed open and in marched none other than the newly appointed head of village homeland security, 'Mateo the Knife.'

He was not alone. On both his left and right hand side stood his henchmen. Both I instantly recognized. Both were rowdies from Spanibont, bullies and thugs I'd once had to hide from in the sand dunes when they were going up and down the beach saying hurtful things to any of the village men fog-bathing in speedos.

The three men stood like mute, muscle bound, badly sculpted statues, awaiting their master's orders. You could have cut the atmosphere in the chamber with a knife.

Then it happened.

Mrs. T simply nodded her head towards old Thomas and barked, "Zero tolerance!"

In an instant the three thugs set upon the aging grave digger and dragged him from the room, slamming the doors closed behind them. We could hear the old man's pathetic, wheezy screams fading into the night as we all turned our eyes towards Mrs. T. After an interminably long silence, I was the first to speak.

"What will happen to him?"

Mrs. T eyed me coldly, and with a sneer on her face she said, "He will be separated from his parents and thrown into a cage. His parents will then be charged with a criminal offense of my choice then sent back to where the buggers came from."

Where does she get these insane ideas from?

Old Thomas' parents are both in their nineties! The two of them live in the sheltered accommodation for 'out of date-code' villagers in the wooden houses on stilts provided by the council at Bogbourne. Further, they were each born and bred in Llanaber.

I said nothing.

I instinctively understood what was happening. Another bandwagon was being jumped on by Mrs. Trim, but for once, in this case, it was not the cheese ball headed anorexia denier Donald Trump's 'bright idea' that was being plagiarized. Mrs. T had seen the admiration that was oozing from every orifice of the wanabee brutal dictator Trump for the soccer-ball headed lipstick wearing despot, Chinaman Kim Jong Un.

It was obvious. Mrs. T 'wants some.'

If Chinaman Kim can create an oppressive brutal dynasty in North Korea, then why shouldn't she do likewise in Llanaber? She's just as fat if not fatter than him, and her hairdo is even worse than his.

Further, she would be stealing the march on the Duck by doing it here before he does it in America.

Whatever, it spells bad news for old Thomas, his folks, the village, and if history is anything to go by, poor old Mrs. Clinton who runs the card shop.

All I'll say is AMERICA BEWARE!

Don't let the Duck do to your democracy what Mrs. Trim is doing to ours.

That's it for now.

Cheerio!

U-TURN IN LLANABER! END OF ZERO TOLERANCE POLICY

Some good news from the village for once. The late (thank heavens) lady Prime Minister of Great Britain and Northern Ireland, Margaret Thatcher, once said, "The lady's not for turning." Not so here in Llanaber.

Yesterday Mrs. Dorothy 'Binky' Trim, the boss of the parish council, called an extra ordinary council meeting at midnight. When we were all assembled, and I must confess, trembling in our seats (the old bag's gone a bit dangerously potty recently) she made the following announcement, and I quote verbatim:

"I have decided to reverse the recently introduced zero tolerance policy towards illegal immigration and anybody that dares defy me. I have ordered the head of village homeland security, Mateo the knife, to release old Thomas from the cage I had hastily erected behind the swings in the school playground. Further I've also released Thomas' parents from the village clink and given them each a £1 coin for their bus fare back to Bogbourne with the proviso they sign one of *Solly's special 'non-disclosure no comebacks' agreements, which they have both done."

My 'fruit loop' of a leader then went on to say with venom, "It was all old mother Clinton's fault. When will people realize what an evil old cow she is, and what's more she's a crook! There is NO extra butter in her fudge. I've seen the recipe."

The sycophants and toadies in the council chamber rather embarrassingly immediately started banging their chairs and chanting 'lock her up.'

After about five minutes chanting, Mrs. T raised her hand, a signal for them to stop. She then eyeballed the councillors and said, and again I quote verbatim:

"Old mother Clinton wants open borders between us and Spanibont, let all the rowdies come in, let them pour in... She doesn't care about the impact of uncontrolled rowdies on your communities your schools, your hospitals, your jobs or your safety. She puts rowdies before Llanaber citizens, what the hell is going on?"

It was then I noticed it. As she spoke, she kept glancing down at her hands. She was slowly trailing a string of ticker tape through her fingers and reading what was written on it as she spoke. These were not her words. These were not her original thoughts. Some other idiot had made them up first. In a flash I knew beyond a shadow of a doubt Mrs. T had raided the waste bin in the news feed room. I decided there and then to get a padlock for the ticker tape room door.

The old girl thundered on;

"With immediate effect I am re-allocating the homeland security team to form a new special force, the village 'Protection from Extra Terrestrials Service.' I've reallocated funds from the village hospital budget to buy them each a silver 'onesie' with the logo 'PETS' printed across the chest. They will patrol the village 24/7 hunting down all the undocumented extra-terrestrials, ripping their kids from the parents' tentacles and throwing them into the cage behind the swings. The green skinned, bug eyed parents will then be fired from the village catapult back to where they came from."

She added while surreptitiously reading from the ticker tape, "We have the air force, but now we're going to have the space force, the PETS. We need it! We need it!"

I very nearly raised my hand to point out we don't actually have an air force, but thought better of it. I'm not entirely convinced her zero tolerance policy is over and I didn't want to give Mrs. T an excuse to accuse me of being an extra-terrestrial.

When the meeting was over I nipped up to the ticker tape machine. There I rummaged through the waste bin. Yes, there was a strip of tape with a chunk missing. It was the report on the cheese-ball headed anorexia denier Donald Trump's rally in Minnesota. I read what was left of the report and quite honestly believe that Mrs. T had plagiarized the only sane part of his speech.

*Solly Weinstein (no relation) Mrs. Trim's lawyer, the village amateur video maker and pervert, has a 'special form' he makes people he has over a barrel fill in and sign. This entitles Solly not only to what is required of the signatory but also a free go on any females involved.

It came through on the US news feed that as the Duck and his entourage entered Speaker Ryan's office in the Capitol, someone on the other side of the Capitol rotunda, they suspect a male intern, yelled, 'Mr. President, F—k you!'

What is it about Mr. Trump that people think is so sexy?

I must confess, I can't see it. To me he just looks like an orange headed fat bloke with a terrible comb over, tiny hands, and a mouth he can make look like a Chimp's butt. Not so to this particular young man, obviously. But the callow youth can't have been familiar with the courtship rituals of those of the 'differently ugly-bumpers' (DUBs) persuasion. You don't just yell out, 'Hey sexy! I want to f---k you!' DUB courtship is more subtle than that.

Also, the young lad should be aware that, while this particular President is easy going when it comes to sexual harassment in the workplace, the law nowadays comes down like a ton of bricks on foul-mouthed horny cretins like him.

Having said that I was very surprised that, in these enlightened modern times of 'Me Too' back-shafting the powerful that made you rich, the legal eagle and consigliore from the Godfather, Rudi Giuliani was never prosecuted.

Why?

For making public his now famous sexual desires towards Chinaman Kim, saying that he wanted to see (Kim) 'on his hands and knees begging for it.' I suppose that because Chinaman Kim is a foreigner, Giuliani's homoerotic comments don't count.

So, my advice to the young lad hanging about on the rotunda for a glimpse of his sex fantasy is to take a box of tissues to the restroom and get the President out of your system. He's way out of your league. Also, he's married to the beautiful gastric banded 'lingerie model potential' robot-faced Melanie. Further, Trump may not be of the DUB preference (although he does allegedly hold men's hand in public, especially French men).

If you can't, then get another job, or keep your loud face-cave shut and stop embarrassing your President with your unwanted sexual advances. As a last resort try popping round to see 'Old Harv.' He's always frisky and not that particular nowadays.

That's it for now.

Cheerio!

BORDER VISIT BY LEADER'S SPOUSE THWARTS ALIEN INVASION

I was unfortunate enough to have been with Mrs. Dorothy Binky' Trim in the café on the sea front having a quick cup of tea when who should walk through the door but none other than Mrs. Winfrey, the official village gossip. Despite not being invited she came right up to join us.' As soon as her fat butt had settled on the seat next to Mrs. T's she came out with the following, and I quote verbatim:

"Did you hear that Melanie Trump has joined the space cadets and has been sent to Russia to get pregnant by a footballer for a lifetime's free burger supply, but she can't get back into America because she keeps her undocumented kids in a cage?"

Of course I knew it was all untrue. However, Mrs. T's eyes lit up, "Free burgers for life, you say?"

"Yes, but no soft drinks," replied the wrinkly old gossip.

I quickly moved Mrs. T on to what I believed the true stories were, once separated from the conflated verbal vomit spewed out by 'wander-brain' Winfrey.

Of the three stories, Mrs. T homed in on the one concerning Donald Trump's gastric banded robot faced wife, Melanie.

"I believe her visit to the Mexican border to see how illegal immigrant children are being looked after is being broadcast live on the TV as we speak," I told her.

"Then let's get to a telly," she said.

Unfortunately, on that day the perpetual fog had lifted and there was a TV signal. Together we watched as the 'lingerie model potential' wife of the President sat bored stiff, pretending to be interested and, after painfully long silences, asking inane questions like 'do they eat stuff?' and 'do any of them have cloven hooves?'

Mrs. T could not draw her eyes from the set. When the embarrassing PR stunt at last came to an end, Mrs. T slammed her fist on the table and barked, "It should have been me!"

She went on to say that 'Mel the Belle' had pulled off the PR stunt of the century turning defeat into victory, reversing all the bad press her chubby-hubby was getting by foregoing her face exfoliation that day to schlep down to Mexico and sit about looking as if she actually cared. Simply brilliant!

"Why?" I asked in all innocence.

She looked at me with her cold eyes and said, "Kids and puppies, dolt!"

I understood straight away. Anything that looks as if you care about these two things is a surefire PR winner. There is an election coming at the end of the summer, and I know Mrs. T has been racking her brains for a deadly certain PR story to bolster her waning popularity.

Now, since the disastrous experiment earlier this month to improve safety in our schools by arming the five-year-olds with knuckledusters, Mrs. T has been scared of school-kids. So it was no surprise when she barked out a string of orders at me concerning puppies. Her instructions were as follows:

"Take some cash from the village hospital budget then go to the pet shop in Druidellau and buy ten puppies. Stick 'em in a suitcase. Take 'em all to the clifftop on the border with Spanibont. Hide in the bushes and wait for me there."

"Why?" I asked.

"Because Leonard is going to rescue them in front of the world's press! I'll call you on my cell phone to let you know precisely when to let them out of the suitcase."

With that she had gone off to organize Leonard's part in her little ruse, no doubt. She disappeared off at such speed that I didn't have the chance to point out the obvious flaws in her evil plan.

Firstly, there isn't a pet shop in Druidellau. The nearest one is in Spanibont but it only sells sheep.

Secondly, were anyone able to contact the 'world press' I can't see that they would be interested in covering a 'fake news' story about puppies being rescued on the Llanaber / Spanibont border. As scoops go, this would rank alongside 'man found dead in graveyard' or 'vandals steal wheel off abandoned stroller.' The best that could be achieved at short notice is the village newsletter. But as I write that I would have to be hiding in the bushes with a suitcase full of puppies, that's a complete non-starter.

Thirdly, Leonard is a human disaster when it comes to dexterity. He is obese, half blind and dyspraxic. Let him loose near puppies on the clifftop and he'll trip on one, roll over and flatten the rest then plummet over the cliff edge to an early death on the jagged rocks below.

Last, but not least, I don't have a cell phone. The only person who owns a cell phone in the village is Mrs. Trim herself, but it's useless. The village doesn't have any cell phone signal coverage. However, we have been promised by the county council that it is expected to be available within the next 20 years. The puppies will have grown old and died before Mrs. T can call me with the order to set them free.

The secret to all successful disasters is in delegation. I ran as quickly as I could to the school playground. I was lucky. I arrived just in the nick of time. Old Thomas the gravedigger (honorary) was just being released from the hastily assembled cage behind the swings. As he was dusting himself off and signing Solly's crippling NDA, I nodded politely to him while tugging on Mateo the Knife's sleeve. You may recall Mateo has recently been appointed head of the new village space force, 'Protection from Extra Terrestrials Service (PETS).' Mateo followed me over to a secluded spot underneath the slide with a perplexed look on his face.

"Mrs. T has a very special project for you," I told him. Then I tapped the side of my nose and said, "Hush-hush, top secret!"

His eyes lit up like fog-lamps as I told him his new mission.

I modified Mrs. T's original plan thus:

Mateo was to steal ten sheep from the field over the border in Spanibont. He was to paint them all green and tie bunches of twigs to their heads to look like antlers. Then he was to take them to the headland and set them free as soon as he spotted the massive bulk of Leonard Trim wobbling towards the cliff edge. Then he was to leap out, wave his arms in the air and chase the sheep back across the border into Spanibont shouting, "Well done Leonard. You've thwarted this invasion. These undocumented alien deer / sheep hybrids from space are too scared of your wife, Mrs. Dorothy 'Binky' Trim, to illegally settle in Llanaber."

The guy is as dumb as a brick (where have I heard that phrase before?). He didn't even question the ridiculous orders. Like Trump's skinny daughter in front of a camera he trotted off, grinning like a chimp, to buy a pot of green paint before heading for Spanibont to do a spot of rustling.

For my part, I grabbed my camera, notebook, and pencil, then made my way at a leisurely pace towards the border clifftop.

Why?

To cover the event for the world press, of course.

That's it for now.

Cheerio!

PR STUNT DISASTER FOLLOWS TROUSER SLOGAN NIGHTMARE!

First lady Melania Trump boards a plane at Andrews Air Force Base, Md., Thursday, June 21, 2018, to travel to Texas. (AP/Andrew Harnik)

It is often the smallest of details that can turn a PR victory into an unmitigated disaster. This is certainly the case for President Trump's 'not quite living in the real world' wife, the robot-faced Melanie. Her trip to the Mexican border to sit around pretending to care was a master stroke had it not been for the unbelievably stupid coat she wore to travel down there.

What a dufus!

Unfortunately, I have a similar story to tell. You may recall that I was given instructions by the boss of the parish council, Mrs. Dorothy 'Binky' Trim, to fake some news. To cut a long story short, I was to arrange for Mateo the Knife, the head of PETS, the new space force in Llanaber, to steal ten sheep from across the Spanibont border, paint them green, tie twigs to their heads and hide them on the clifftop next to the Llanaber / Spanibont borderline. There he was to hide in the bushes and await the arrival of Mrs. T's roly-poly husband, Leonard. As soon as the lard-butted spouse of my esteemed leader approached the clifftop, Mateo was to leap out and scare the green sheep back across the border into Spanibont, while shouting loudly about how Leonard had 'saved Llanaber from the illegal immigration of undocumented extra-terrestrial deer / sheep hybrids.' I was to cover the event for the world press.

Unbelievably, everything went like clockwork. This ridiculous ruse worked like a charm. Mateo had done a first class job with the sheep, although his choice of gloss paint as opposed to matte paint wasn't his smartest move. The false antlers, on the other hand looked very convincing, though yet again, I think it was a mistake to nail them onto the sheep's heads.

All in all, the event was carried out both convincingly and successfully. I took plenty of photos, wrote the thing up for the village newsletter and published it this morning, popping up at the village and slipping a copy of the newsletter through every letterbox.

So it was a shock when Mrs. T burst into my office, slapped a copy of the article onto my desk and yelled at me, "WHAT THE HELL!"

She was pointing at the photograph I had taken of her pear-shaped spouse's rear end as he wobbled up the hill towards the clifftop.

I picked up the newsletter. I studied it carefully. I could see no problem.

"What?" I stupidly asked.

"Look at his BUTT, you moron!" she screeched at me.

I picked up my magnifying glass and studied the photograph more closely. It was then that I saw what was wrong. My heart sank. I had erred. But in my defense it wasn't my fault. It was her husband, the idiot Leonard, who had decided on that day of all days to wear his 'jocular keks.' Leonard has several pairs of trousers that he names. Each pair has a 'comedy slogan' printed in luminous ink on the seat of the trousers. In the photograph the slogan was clearly visible. I reproduce it for you verbatim.

The slogan read:

'I COULDN'T GIVE A FART! COULD YOU?'

Leonard's trousers are vast across the butt. The phrase was written in one single line starting at the far left of his left butt cheek, and finishing on the far right of his right.

I pride myself on being professional, so I felt humbled in front of my esteemed leader for my massive, unforgivable error. I also knew that the mistake was irreversible. It was too late to recall the newsletter. The photo was already in the public domain. Further, there would now be no chance that we could re-create the little vignette at the clifftop. As soon as the green painted, twig antlered sheep were driven back into Spanibont, the poor uneducated ignoramus over there killed them all, thinking they were a new breed of sheep that combined both the meat and the vegetables into one animal. They would now be all gone, served up in a paint flavored mutton stew of some sort, no doubt.

I just thank my lucky stars I didn't publish the photographs I had of Leonard taken from the front. Across the crotch of his novelty trousers that day was printed the phrase:

'Who gives a toss? NOT ME!'

There has been a 'development' following the imprisonment of old Thomas the gravedigger (honorary). You may recall Mrs. T had Thomas bundled from yesterday's parish council meeting by her new space patrol henchman, Mateo the Knife, for showing descent, i.e. pointing out she was drinking cold tea, not coffee.

The poor old duffer was taken to the village school playground and thrown into the cage that Mrs. T had hastily erected there. Old Thomas has now been 'pardoned' and released. But while he was incarcerated the Druidian paparazzi must have been tipped off. A video has emerged of old Thomas sitting in the cage sucking his thumb and asking passers-by for a chicken sandwich. The Druids would do anything to blacken the character of our council, even though Mrs. T is as thick as thieves with their leader, Benjy Yahoo. There has been a long standing enmity between the two councils ever since we asked them to clean up the blood, limbs and dog-shit from the beach after a particularly heavy 're-education' session of the Travelers' kids by the Druids' henchmen.

There will no doubt be a scandal. The village will be portrayed in a terrible light on the world stage. I must confess the sight of old Thomas in the video, sobbing and pleading for a coronation chicken wrap, brought tears to my eyes.

As I write this newsletter I have just received a note tied to a magazine, tied to a brick that has just been thrown through my window. I will deal with each in turn.

The brick: At first glance this appeared to be a brick shaped chunk of Bara Brith, a confection made from bread ingredients and sawdust popular with the villagers which has the specific gravity of lead. On closer examination it was not. It was, in fact, concentrated devil-dog-shit compressed into a brick shape.

The magazine: This is a copy of the weekly gardening magazine published by the Druids called 'THYME.' On the front cover was a cleverly mocked up photo. This shows Mrs. T standing upright against a scarlet background. Unfortunately the photo they used is the one of her when she attended the Druids' 'not-Christmas' fancy dress ball when she went dressed as Adolf Hitler. She is looking down upon old Thomas, reduced in size so he looks child-like. He is crying, and has his thumb in his mouth. Superimposed over this is a picture of her hastily erected cage. The strap-line to the picture reads: 'Welcome to Llanaber.'

The note: It consisted of letters cut out from a magazine and pasted onto a small sheet of paper. The message reads as follows:

"Start bad mouthing the Travelers or we publish the mag and upload the vid to YouTube."

It was signed, 'A Friend' but I suspect it's from the Druids.
What the hell's a YouTube?
Whatever it is it spells more trouble for the village, I'm sure.
That's it for now.
Cheerio!

'HUMAN MISERY PARADE' PR STUNT ATTEMPT TO OFFSET BAD PRESS

Steve (Reeno) Kloser @reeno317

I suspect that the boss of Llanaber parish council, Mrs. Dorothy 'Binky' Trim has caught on to my ploy to censor the news by tearing out great lumps of ticker tape from the parish office's news feed before Mrs. T sees them. I was busy 'censoring' this morning, completely absorbed in my work, when the door of the 'coms room' crashed open. There stood Mrs. T (well, more crouched really. Mrs.T is six feet tall and the ticker tape ceiling is only five feet off the floor). Her new henchman and head of the newly formed village 'space cadets' (PETS) Mateo the knife, was by her side. They both glared daggers at me.

Her surprise raid had been too quick for me. While I quickly stuffed the piece of ticker tape I had in my hand at the time into my mouth and started chewing rapidly, Mateo was on me in a flash. His vice like grip ceased my jaws. In mere moments, the snippet of news I was trying to suppress was in my esteemed leader's hands. Regardless of the saliva, she unfurled it and read the story. Her face broke out into a wicked grin. I'd seen that look before. It always spells trouble for the village.

So, what was the news item I had tried to hide from the bandwagon jumping boss of the village council? (I hear you cry). I reproduce the headline to the article for you below:

"TRUMP GATHERS ALIEN-VIOLENCE VICTIMS TO TRASH MEDIA'S SNATCHED BABY BORDER POLICY COVERAGE"

The article went on to describe the utterly crass and cringe-worthy PR stunt pulled by the amber faced anorexia denier in which he lined up a group of US citizens who had all suffered bereavements through illegals' violence and paraded them in front of the world's media. As if this wasn't offensive enough, it was reported that he then started going along the line hugging them one by one. The article makes no mention of whether or not any of the poor citizens were dribbled on (as per Kelly Craft) and subsequently vomited.

"Nice try, weasel-pants!" Mrs. Trim barked at me. Then she turned to Mateo and whispered in his ear. I feared that instructions for a new 'hush hush' special project were being given to the ex-Spanibont boss of the rowdies. It didn't take long before my fears were confirmed. Moments after Mateo ran from the room, Mrs. T turned to me and yelled, "You! Short-house! Run and get your camera!"

I was ordered to summon up the world's press, gather them in the village church hall and await further instructions.

"Why?" I foolishly asked.

"For a world expose," she said (I think she meant exposé).

Before I could once again explain to the old bat that as far as Llanaber was concerned, unless a nuclear bomb landed here, the worlds' press is not in the least bit interested, she had turned on her heels and gone.

I did as I was ordered. I hung around with my camera in the village church hall trying to look like a crowd of news hungry media hounds. In about an hour Mateo turned up, pushing in front of him a befuddled bunch of villagers. They were all what we refer to in the village as 'out of date-coders' (senior citizens to you).

The poor addle-brained elderly people were pushed, threatened, cajoled, bullied, and eventually physically lifted and carried onto the small stage at the back of the hall. As soon as they were in something that resembled a straight line, Mrs. T appeared, wearing her official garb and carrying a megaphone. She stepped onto the stage and turned to face the media pack (me).

Despite the fact that I was standing less than three feet away from her she started yelling at me through the megaphone. I repeat what she yelled for you below verbatim: "Thank you for coming at such short notice, you scumbag fake news pedaling, lying bunch of left-wing subversive establishment tools. For once I have a story that is real news! You'll laugh, you'll cry, it'll change your life. You see standing loosely in a line behind me a picture of human misery. These people have all suffered. How, I hear you cry? I'll tell you. They have suffered the humiliation and ignominy of having the proverbial piss ripped out of them by those ruffians, the rowdies from Spanibont… And when I say ruffians I am, of course, meaning potential rapists, drug dealers, and rapists! Not to mention the drug dealing."

It was only then I noticed the poor old buggers were each holding up a placard, breakfast cereal boxes turned inside out, on which various messages had been written using Mrs. T's crimson lipstick.

Mrs. T turned round and barked at the old duffers, "Hold your cards up for the press you old gits!" This they duly did.

I read the first few then lost heart. While it was undoubtedly the truth that was written on these placards it was of no interest to anyone else in the world but the specific 'auld'un' themselves. I reproduce for you a few examples of what was written on the placards:

'They took the rise out of my speedos!'

'When I was fog-bathing in my bikini they said I looked wrinkly.'

'They said it wasn't worth the effort of kicking sand in my face.'

'They said my knees were more knobbly than Dai's scabby donkeys''

'One of them asked for a lick of my ice cream.'

'I'd forgotten who I was and they wouldn't tell me.'

Mrs. T stepped forward till she was inches from my face then yelled into the megaphone, "Stick that in your newsletter, slimeball!"

I think my esteemed and completely mental leader's plan is to have a good news story like the suffering of these poor old idiots as a counter balance to the bad press following the 'old Thomas in a cage' debacle, and the 'jocular trousers slogans' scandal.

Let's hope the wizard of PR in America, Donald Trump, has more success with his nauseating 'parade of the suffering' than Mrs. T is likely to have with her effort. I should think so. He's the master when it comes to judging the mood of his people and what the right thing to do is to get public opinion on his side.

Did I hear his gastric banded 'lingerie model potential' wife, Melanie, goes to bed in 'onesie pajamas' with the slogan 'Black Lives – Who Cares?' printed on them? (A gift from her husband's KKK supporters). Or is this more scumbag media fake news?

That's it for now.

Cheerio!

SARAH SANDERS EJECTION FROM RESTAURANT IMPACTS LLANABER

Bad news! The boss of the paris council in Llanaber, Mrs. Dorothy 'Binky' Trim, has worked a flanker on me. She has had builders in overnight and knocked the wall through from her office into the news feed ticker tape room, A door has been erected so she can come and go from her office into the ticker tape room whenever she wants.

Further, she has had the existing door bricked up! This means that the only access to the news ticker tape feed is through Mrs. Trim's office. In my opinion this is another step towards North Korea style totalitarian control of information. She has long been an admirer of the cheese-ball headed anorexia denier and brainiac, Donald Trump, but of late, both have turned their admiration and envious eyes towards regimes in the east.

While Mr. Trump hasn't yet said in public of both Russia and North Korea 'at least the trains run on time,' he has chosen to turn a blind eye to human rights and freedom of speech issues in both these countries.

In recent assertions, he has proved he is an overt admirer of Chinaman Kim's control of the North Korean media. If America isn't on the ball then it won't be long before the US too will have Kim style little lists of 'do's and don'ts' rules (e.g. DO clap like a gibbon and anything that comes out of my big fat mouth including a burp, and DON'T think I won't have you, your friends, and your family fed through a mincer if you fail to worship me.)

That's all well and good for the super-states, but what if totalitarianism takes hold here in Llanaber?

Is something giving you cause for concern? (I hear you ask).

Yes. Let me fill you in with the circumstances.

When I tried to sneak past my esteemed leader this morning to get to the ticker tape machine, Mrs. T was sitting at her desk, her nose buried in a string of tape. I was almost past her and into the ticker tape room when she grabbed me by the arm and pushed me onto the tiny stool in front of her desk. (FYI – Mrs. T likes to play power games with people that visit her office. To this end she has replaced the standard chair with a milking stool 'Dai the Sheep' uses when his ewes are lactating. When you sit on it you can't see over the top of the desk).

"You!" she barked down at me, "What do you make of this?"

Moments later the string of tape she was reading fluttered down onto my lap. I read the news item. My heart sank. I knew what was coming next. 'Events' had happened yesterday in the village and old Mrs. Winfrey, the official village gossip, was quick to collar me as I cycled in to work to tell me the story. Admittedly she got it completely wrong as usual, but I 'got the gist' from what she said. What the old windbag told me was as follows and I repeat it verbatim:

"Did you hear that Leonard (Mrs. T's husband) was thrown out of Trevor 'the Trots' Trattoria last night for being an undocumented illegal space invader and smearing unidentified Russian substances on Trevor's toilet door?"

The actual news was something entirely different, of course, but I could see the relevance to the incident with Leonard in Llanaber, and the article Mrs. T had just given me. The news item was about the White House Press Secretary and inflatable fun balloon, Sarah Huckleberry Hound Sanders. She claimed to have been thrown out of the Red Hen restaurant in Lexington, Virginia on the grounds that she occasionally worked for Donald Trump. Stephanie Wilkinson, the owner of the café was quoted as saying, "I would have done the same thing again. We just felt there are moments in time when
people need to live their convictions. This
appeared to be one." Mrs. T stood up so she
could see me.
"This sort of thing is anti-democratic!" she shouted at me,
"And I'm not having it!"

I pointed out that Lexington, Virginia isn't anywhere near Llanaber. So it's out of her jurisdiction. It isn't even in Gwynedd county, or Wales, or Britain.

"I know that, you dolt!" she bellowed, "I'm referring to what happened in the village to poor old Leonard yesterday."

She went on to tell me the story about Leonard, which was as follows.

Yesterday Mrs. T's blubby-hubby, Leonard, broke the scales in the village chemist's shop. That morning before he took his morning constitutional (his walk next door to buy a cake) he'd struggled to make it into his trousers. Mrs. T had watched him unsuccessfully wriggling for twenty-minutes, gave him a 20p coin and ordered him to get his enormous lardy butt down to the chemist's shop to use the public scales.

"I want to know the truth!" she barked at him. (He'd been telling her he was fifteen stone since their engagement forty years ago).

Unfortunately, the chemist's shop scales only go up to thirty stone. When Leonard stepped on, the spring flew out and ruined a display of suppositories.

Mrs. T went ballistic when Mrs. Walgreen, the old girl that owns the chemist's shop, started demanding money from the parish council to fix the broken scales.

She barked at Leonard, "As of now you're on a low carbs, low fat, no alcohol, tissues only diet!"

It is a matter of record that in the last thirty years Leonard hasn't gone without food for more than six minutes. Even when he goes to bed he has a tube in his mouth connected to a vat of chicken fat so he can snore and swallow at the same time.

There is only one business in town that can be remotely classified as a restaurant, Trevor's Trattoria.

Under normal circumstances Trevor 'the Trots' cafe is 'out of bounds' for Leonard. It only opens from ten in the morning till noon, after which it closes for lunch for the rest of the day. Leonard is normally working in Mrs. T's sweet shop then. But, due to acute pain brought on by hunger pains, Leonard 'took off work' and went across the road, avoiding the massive sink hole, to partake of Trevor's 'all you can eat spaghetti buffet.' (FYI- This is just spaghetti).

I'm sure, dear reader, you can fill in the gaps yourself, but suffice to say, Trevor watched as the fat glutton wired into the buffet and hoovered the place clean of food. Once Leonard had cleaned up the buffet, he then started scraping the food off the plates of the only other diners in there, a Mexican family on a camping holiday.

Trevor could stand it no longer.

He bundled the fat glutton out of his restaurant, and slammed the door closed behind him. Trevor then apologized to the Mexicans saying, "I would do the same thing again. I just felt there are moments in time when people need to live their convictions and bundle fat pig-monsters like him away from the 'all you can eat' section of my cafe. This appeared to be one."

At the next parish council meeting, Mrs. T intends to put forward a motion to impose tariffs on pasta products brought into the village for resale to the tune of 1,000,000%. This would put poor old Trevor out of business, for sure.

In 1867 John Stuart Mills famously said, "Bad men need nothing more to compass their ends, than that good men should look on and do nothing." How right he was.

I believe I am a man of principle, a 'good man.'

Even if I stand alone in the council chambers, I will vote against this wicked, petty and punitive motion Mrs. T intends to have enacted in the village, its sole purpose to ruin another 'good man's' business. In years to come I will, with a clear conscience, look my Grandchildren squarely in the eye and tell them 'I did my bit' to stem the rise of totalitarianism in Llanaber.

It helps that Trevor offered me a bribe in the form of free goes at his lunchtime buffet for life if I stop the old cow from doing it.

That's it for now.

Cheerio!

TRUMP HITS NEW LOW WITH TOM SELLECK QUIP

I have to report being gobsmacked by a news item that came through on the village news feed ticker tape this morning. I was lucky to be first to get to the news room as the boss of the village parish council, Mrs. Dorothy 'Binky' Trim, was having a little 'zizz' at her desk and I managed to crawl past without waking her.

The story concerned Mr. Trump's bumpy 'zero tolerance' immigration policy, and the unbelievable 'sick fest' cabaret Trump conjured up to counterbalance the appalling worldwide revulsion to it.

The recently abandoned zero tolerance modus operandi was perfectly sensible in my opinion. It was to rip children from the arms of undocumented illegals, throw the parents into prison, and the kids into cages for a couple of days to scare 'em up a bit. When they were thoroughly terror stricken they were then scattered across the US to God knows where, never to be found again.

What was wrong with that?

The poor little mites had probably never travelled that much before, and it'd be a nice change for them to eat something other than chili. What's more, if they ended up being fostered by a white family, they automatically moved several rungs up the social ladder. (The converse for a black one, though – hey, but life's a lottery, yeah?)

Anyway, the leftie, pinko, live-on-your-knees, thumb-sucking liberal sandals-shufflers around the world all thought it was a bad idea. They don't want these under-privileged kids to get a better life so they kicked up a fuss.

The upshot was the amber soccer-ball headed brainiac comb-over reacted to quash the bad PR by sending his gastric banded 'lingerie model potential' robot faced wife, Melanie down south to pretend she cared. But she screwed up by wearing a jacket with 'Bugger You, I'm Rich,' or something similar printed on the back. So the stunt backfired.

'What to do? What to do?' thought the President, 'I know. I'll dig out a dozen or so 'active grievers,' i.e. those that had their loved ones knocked off by those nasty illegals.'

N. B. In his soccer-ball shaped head it is axiomatic that if one illegal is a murderer, they must all be. However, peculiarly, and contrary to Trump's mathematical predictions, there have been millions of illegal immigrants over the last 20 years but not millions of murders.

Back to the story…

'Great idea!' thought the President, 'I'll line 'em up on a stage in front of the world's press, each holding up a photo of the loved one they lost. Then (and here's the bit that surprised me) I'll start passing comments about the pictures while signing them!' Unbelievable!

What a PR triumph.

It was reported on the ticker tape that he commented about one victim's picture, and here I quote verbatim:

"This is Tom Selleck, except better looking. Right? Better looking."

What a guy! The family of the deceased gentleman concerned must have gone away from the 'sorry for your loss / I'll pretend to give a toss' PR stunt much more able to cope with the grieving process knowing their murdered son / brother / husband or whatever, bore a passing resemblance to a bit player in 'Friends.'

I just wonder what other comments the president made that the media were too embarrassed to report. My imagination has conjured up the following comments the Duck could have made:

'Keep your pictures. I've signed them. They'll be worth something one day.'

'She's no great loss with a nose like that.'

'Is this him without the stab wound in the eye?'

'You still got other kids, though, right?'

'He looks a bit Mexican. Was this a gang war thing?'

There were also a couple of other news items that caught my eye. The brain dead 'sideways glancer' and angel of death, Jeff Sessions, is doing his best to back track on the zero tolerance undocumented aliens' kid-caging policy screw up. On a Christian TV show he said, and I quote verbatim:

"The American people don't like the idea that we are separating families," he said. "We never really intended to do that." ... 'Never really intended?' Classic!

So it was all just a mishap, a mistake, an unfortunate misunderstanding by the border guards.

"D'aw shucks! I've inadvertently torn that toddler from its mother's arms and throwed it in a cage! Stupid ol' me! Whoops! I just gone dun it agin! Better get all these brown liddle'uns on a bus outa town before someone sees I dun screwed up!" It got better.

I read a piece about the fun balloon, inflatable mouth and restaurant evictee, Sarah 'Huckleberry Hound' Sanders. It read as follows:

'White House Press Secretary Sarah Huckabee Sanders also used the Bible to defend the administration's policies, telling reporters: "I can say that it is very biblical to enforce the law. That is actually repeated a number of times throughout the Bible."'

I think she may have failed to realize that there are a lot of things in the bible, and some of them aren't very nice. Let me suggest a few that the Trump administration would do well to take note of (and make sure the mental sideways-glancer doesn't see these in case he starts quoting them, eh?)

Rev 21: 8 "Liars--their place will be in the fiery lake of burning sulfur.
This is the second death."

Isaiah 13:9–16 NIV "See, the day of the Lord is coming — a cruel day, with wrath and fierce anger. . . . I will put an end to the arrogance of the haughty. . . . Their infants will be dashed to pieces before their eyes; their houses will be looted and their wives violated." Eternal damnation for lying?

Bad news for the haughty?

Watch out Donald!

My personal favorite is for fun-bag Sarah herself:

1 Timothy 2:12 "I do not permit a woman to teach or to have authority over a man; she must be silent."

For a closer on this, Mr. Trump's US administration must be scrabbling around trying to formulate a new 'user-friendly' immigration policy to replace the failed zero tolerance debacle. Can I suggest the team all bear in mind the quote below while doing their brainstorming:

Luke 18: 16 – "But Jesus called them *unto him,* and said, Suffer little children to come unto me, and forbid them not: for of such is the kingdom of God."

It doesn't mention shoving them in cages, does it?

That's it for now. Cheerio!

HUMILIATING ADMIN MEMBERS IN PUBLIC THREATENS NICE LUNCHES ON EXPENSES

Today, it was a terrible start to the day. I was in the bathroom taking care of 'some business' when the whistle went on my 'speaking tube.'

Llanaber has very few telephones and as yet the only person in the village with a cell phone is the boss of the parish council, Mrs. Dorothy 'Binky' Trim. It's of no use to her here as there is no cell phone service in the village, but Gwynedd council has promised coverage before the end of 2038.

So, it's obligatory that every member of the council has a 'speaking tube' fitted in various rooms in their home. The speaking tubes link all the council members' homes and offices together, so we can converse confidentially without interfering busybodies like old Mrs. Winfrey, the official village gossip, listening in. In all honesty, it's an antiquated system we rarely use. The user has to blow into the tube and a whistle is sounded in the home of the person you want to speak to. Usually its main use is as an escape route for the village mice when 'Scratchy Jack' does his annual disinfestation after the leek harvest.

I digress.

The speaking tube whistle alerted me to the fact that someone wanted to speak to me. I knew it must be important as it was only six thirty in the morning, too early for anything other than trouble. It was, but at the time I had no idea of how much. I would find that out soon enough.

The call was from old Thomas the gravedigger (honorary). He had a bad experience that morning and wanted to tell me about it. When he recounted his tale I was lost for words. This is what happened to him.

Old Thomas lives on his own in a cottage at the edge of the village. The cottage is over 200 years old and has no gas, electricity or running water. It doesn't even have a bathroom. Old Thomas, being weak in the bladder, has to get out of bed and shuffle up to the public conveniences in the main street every time he needs to answer 'a call of nature.' This he may have to do up to ten times a night. It's a hazardous enterprise for two reasons, one being the enormous sink hole filled with garbage in the middle of the high street which Thomas, only being half awake, has fallen into several times, and the other being the law. Thomas doesn't have time to get dressed so he pops to the public loo in just his onesie. It's a frequent occurrence that his 'John Thomas' has been spotted peeping out to see the sun rise, and several of the village maidens have complained. Our village cop, Robert 'Robbie the Bobbie' Muller has put old Thomas on his last warning, i.e. if it happens again he'll be on a community service order to clean daily for three months the very facility he uses up to ten times a night.

The perpetual fog had lifted last night and there was TV signal. Old Thomas had stayed up late watching the Russian world cup and (foolishly) enjoying a couple of beers. The consequences were obvious. He was up and down all night like the proverbial whore's undergarments. All his trips had passed without incident except for the one at six. He was shuffling his way around the rim of the sink hole when he bumped into 'Dai the Milk,' the village dairyman, on his morning round of deliveries. Dai is an easy going person and normally the most convivial of chaps.

Not so this morning. The moment Dai spotted old Thomas creeping gingerly round the rim of the sink hole in his onesie clutching his privates, he started berating him. It was right there in the street in full view of the public.

He pointed his finger at old Thomas and bellowed, "You're not welcome – anymore, anywhere – we've got to get the children connected to their parents, the children are suffering." Can you imagine the shock?

Right there in the street, at six o'clock in the morning, the aged parish councillor was being 'called out' by the village milkman. It was too much for old Thomas' bladder and he had to run all the way home in his pee-sodden onesie. I could hear his voice quivering when the old chap told me his tale down the speaking tube. I offered my commiserations and hung up by putting the whistle back in the tube.

I was flummoxed!

I had no idea why the village dairyman would have behaved like this. The most aggressive I've ever seen Dai the Milk previously was when his cousin, Dai the Sheep restricted his supply of ewe's milk in a failed attempt to manipulate the ewe's milk market to force the price up. Even then all he said was, "You wouldn't think the old git was my cousin."

Later, while I was cycling to work pondering on old Thomas' story, a similar, very unsettling thing happened to me. As I was parking my bicycle in the parish bike rack, old Mrs. Winfrey waddled over towards me. She held her arm out and pointed an aggressive index finger at me and shouted for the entire world to hear, and I quote her words verbatim:

"You're not welcome – anymore, anywhere – we've got to get the children connected to their parents, the children are suffering."

They were the exact same words Dai the Milk had spat out at poor old Thomas!

What was going on?

I was once again flummoxed.

I backed away from the bulky gossip and made a bolt for the sanctuary of the parish council office building entrance. But before I reached its safety, my path was blocked by none other than the man that owns the amusement arcade on the seafront, the 'beast from the east,' Putin Lotzadosh. He held his arm out towards me, pointed an accusing finger and yelled at the top of his voice, "You're not welcome – anymore, anywhere – we've got to get the children connected to their parents, the children are suffering."

I barged past the 'baldy Balkan' and ran inside the building, slamming the door behind me. I made my way straight to the news feed ticker tape room. Mrs. Trim was already there. She said nothing. She just held out her arm towards me. I cringed. Was she too going to berate me with this bizarre phrase that seemed to be on everyone's lips?

No.

Instead, in her hand was a string of news ticker tape. I took it from her and read it slowly. The article's headline was as follows:

'Congresswoman Maxine Waters calls for attacks on Trump administration.'

It went on to quote what the Congresswoman had said at a recent rally, "If you see anybody from that (Trump's) cabinet in a restaurant, in a department store, at a gasoline station, you get out and you cause a crowd, and you push back on them, and you tell them they're not welcome – anymore, anywhere – we've got to get the children connected to their parents, the children are suffering."

The perpetual fog in my head lifted. I understood. There had been TV signal last night. News of what Congresswoman Waters had said must have reached the village. Some smart Alec had started a campaign to humiliate all Mrs. T's councillors for what she had done in her recent campaign of zero tolerance, especially the cruel and unjustifiable separation of kids from their parents and throwing them in cages.

Campaigns such as this (the humiliation of councillors, not the zero tolerance one – that seems sensible to me) are typical ill-informed populist show boating, headline grabbing, leftie, pinko claptrap perpetrated by the thumb sucking wets out to cause trouble.

As far as Llanaber is concerned, the perpetrators are woefully illinformed. The only ones affected by Mrs. Trim's recent 'ripping kids from their folks' zero tolerance debacle was old Thomas and his family! He was the only one she had thrown into the hastily assembled cage behind the swings in the village school. His parents were the only ones dragged from their 'out of date-coders' retirement home in Bogbourne.

Haven't they suffered enough?

This blatant persecution of the members of the administration both in Llanaber and the US - put there by God himself, if 'sideways glancer' and complete lunatic Jeff Sessions is to be believed - must be stopped, and must be stopped NOW before it gains momentum.

Why? (I hear you ask).

Is it as per Ronna McDaniel, the chair of the US Republican National Committee's recent rally remarks that 'all dissent must be crushed'?

No it is not!

Then is it that it's undemocratic, cheap populism and persecuting 'those in power' that have to make difficult decisions for the greater benefit of society?

No, quite the contrary. I wish the best of luck to anyone trying to oust
the mad old bat we have as our parish leader.

Then what is it? (I hear you ask again).

I get a free go at the 'all you can eat' Spaghetti buffet (it's just spaghetti) at Trevor the Trots' Trattoria this lunchtime. I don't want any old hobbledehoy coming over yelling at me in the café and spoiling my lunch.

That's it for now. Cheerio!

DRUNKEN BLAB REVEALS PUTIN'S SECRET 'MASTER PLAN' FOR AMERICA

The image was originally posted to Flickr by Don Irvine Photos at https://flickr.com/photos/60661112@N00/5104952894

What I thought was going to be a quiet lunch in Trevor the Trots' local café today turned into a nightmare. It wasn't that what I was afraid would happen, happened, i.e. one of the villagers pointing at me and screaming, 'You're not welcome – anymore, anywhere – we've got to get the children connected to their parents, the children are suffering.' It was something far more sinister. Let me set the scene for you.

At ten o'clock in the morning (lunchtime in Llanaber) I donned a false beard and dark glasses, and sneaked out of the office and went across the road to Trevor's Trattoria for my free meal, a free go at his 'all you can eat' spaghetti buffet (it's just spaghetti). As I loaded my three plates I looked around

the restaurant for somewhere to sit. There was only one other
diner, a fat man in his sixties, gray mullet, wild crazy eyes. He
was staring at me. As soon as our eyes made contact he waved
me over, shouting, "Come and sit by me y'all!"

He was an American.

This is not unusual for this time of the year in the village.
During the dark days of the leek famines many folk from
Llanaber bailed out on the poverty stricken village and took
the decision to seek their fortune in 'the new world.'

Most of them died of starvation before completing the
Atlantic crossing. Why? (I hear you ask).

Simply this. These poor souls had been raised
exclusively on a diet of leeks (Leek soup, stewed leeks, leek
fricassee, braised leek in leek sauce, leek a la mode, devilled
leeks, leek bourguignon – you get the picture). In those days,
the only food permitted on board a trans-Atlantic vessel was
limes.

However some survived, a number of who went on to
make their fortune, and generations later, although American
citizens, still recognized their roots and humble beginnings.
Hence, occasionally we get the odd Yank in the village,
splashing their cash around, looking down their noses at the
abject poverty most of us still live in and mouthing off about
what a shit-hole Llanaber is. They take a few snaps just to
prove back home that Rickets still exists in the 'old country'
before sodding off to somewhere nicer for the rest of their
vacation. I suspected this chap was one of these.

But I was wrong.

As I took my seat he introduced himself as somebody or
other. He had such an incomprehensible drawl I didn't quite
catch his surname.

"Just call me Stevie," he said, and before I could
introduce myself he launched into a long diatribe. I could only
sit and listen, transfixed by his every word. What he was
saying was political dynamite!

While I can't recount verbatim what the strange fellow
said, this is the general gist.

'Stevie' is a right wing political guru, on a tour of Europe
to, and I can quote verbatim here, 'stir the pot.'

He is on his way to London to meet 'certain politicians' in the cabinet there, the names of whom he would not divulge.

Stevie had just come from a right wing rally in France where he was an invited speaker. This was one of many he had attended as part of his 'bait the hate' European tour.

I gathered by the fact that I hadn't even at this stage been invited to offer my name, let alone enter into a two sided conversation, that 'Stevie' was a narcissistic piece of shit and possibly insane. I feared I was having my lunch break freebee hi-jacked by a 'nut job.' (Where have I heard that phrase before?)

My fears were realized when he started telling me a very chilling tale about his past. But before I do I must mention that 'Stevie' had inadvertently ordered a pint of the local brew known as 'journey into space.' It's a thick brown liquid, not unlike treacle, made from fermented leeks, sheep's hoof trimmings, and dottle. Only tourists are foolish enough to drink the stuff as it's really meant for rubbing into donkey saddles to give them a bit of butt-grip. Apparently it was Stevie's second pint of the stuff, and his tongue had become loose. (I don't mean he was indiscreet, I mean his tongue had literally become loose). This enabled me to better understand his drawling accent.

This is what he told me:

Stevie claimed to be the genius behind the cheese-ball headed anorexia denier and brainiac, Donald Trump's election victory in 2016.

It was an outlandish claim and I immediately took him to task.

"Impossible! This could never happen in a mature democracy. How? Explain?" I demanded.

He stared at me for a moment with a twisted, almost manic expression. Then he tapped the side of his nose with his index finger and said, "Putin!" I was curious.

"Do you mean the gangster that runs the amusement arcade on the sea front here?" I naively asked.

"No!" he barked, now deadly serious, "I mean the gangster that runs
Russia!"

His speech was beginning to slur but I still understood every word.

"Trump's as dumb as a brick," he mumbled (Where have I heard that phrase before), "He'd never've got in without the Ruskies. He owes the Russians. And they've got a video of him with the prostitutes playing the 'golden shower' game on Obama's bed."

I had no idea what he was rambling on about but sat motionless, eyes agog, hanging on his every word.

He continued, "Putin hates America. He hates Europe. He hates anyone that thinks Russia is shit now compared to what it was when he was a kid, the USSR. So, he had a brainwave. Put someone he owns into The White House then break the whole thing to bits."

I asked for an explanation. This is what he said.

"If you were Putin what would you like to happen? How about this, America fighting with its neighbors, Mexico and Canada, America breaking up Nato, America at loggerheads with the European Union, America involved in a pointless trade war, American companies repatriating their businesses back to the US then finding tariffs that stop them from selling their products abroad and making them go bust, Americans fighting themselves, left versus right, blacks versus whites, Hispanics versus everybody, gays versus straights, the establishment versus the electorate…"

His voice trailed off as he started to half laugh, half cry.

"What have I done?" he eventually sobbed through tear stained eyes.

"Do you mean Trump is doing to America what he's denied doing to Stormy Daniels and f…?"

I didn't need to finish my sentence.

He nodded slowly confirming the affirmative.

"… And six months ahead of Putin's schedule," said the strange visitor.

He started to blub harder into his foul smelling treacle colored toxic brew. I stood and quietly slipped out of the café, leaving this broken man to reflect on the folly of his deeds.

I will not sleep soundly tonight.

My dreams will not be filled of the images of what is yet to befall the fate of mankind, if the bloated faced, mullet-headed crackpot, Stevie's claptrap is to be believed.

No, dear reader, after three platefuls of Trevor's Trattoria spaghetti, I defy anyone to get a good night's sleep.

That's it for now.

Cheerio!

TRUMP'S TRAVEL BAN VICTORY IMPACTS LLANABER

The head of the parish council, Mrs. Dorothy 'Binky' Trim, was well ahead of me this morning with the latest news coming off the parish ticker tape feed. When I arrived at work she was already in my office clutching a long string of ticker tape and yelling about.

"Look at this!" she barked, throwing the tape at me.

I slowly read the article in question (I'm not a fast reader). It was an article about the boss of America's travel ban and the recent Supreme Court ruling in Trump's favor.

"So what?" I asked naively.

She went apoplectic.

"Why haven't WE got a travel ban!?" she yelled at me.

It is never wise to 'knee jerk' respond to any batty remark made by my esteemed leader, so I pretended to be thinking hard. I put my fist under my chin, closed my eyes and said, "Hmmmm."

"Stop pretending to think!" she bellowed at me, "This is serious."

Why?

This village has been in existence since 'Plop the Dozy' and his stone-age family dug a hole and started sleeping in it with their sheep 8,000 years ago. In all this time we've neither needed nor wanted a travel ban. I mustered up some courage and asked the obvious question.

"Who would we want to ban? Nobody in their right mind would want to…"

I didn't get to finish my sentence.

"THE BLOODY INCAS!" she yelled at me, "Get off your lazy butt and start banning them, NOW!"

I am not a brave man, so it wasn't easy to openly defy the orders I had just been given, especially as Mrs. T has a long memory and bears grudges. But to impose a travel ban on the Incas would be not only unjust but insane. The tribe no longer exists. If my memory of my school history lessons is correct, Francisco Pizarro and his entourage of mercenaries (conquistadors) killed them off in the sixteenth century. So, I gingerly pointed this out to the crazy old bat.

"Urban myth," she said, "They've changed their name, that's all." I took an educated guess.

"Mexicans?"

"Near enough," she said, "Get them banned, right away!"

I could see the connection her empty pot-hole of a brain had made, but I couldn't see why she had singled out the Mexican tribe for special treatment. I foolishly asked her straight out. What had she got against Mexicans?

"Do I have to 'Janet and John' everything for you, dolt-brain? They're bloody sun worshippers!"

There then followed a convoluted rant that tore logic up into tiny pieces then flushed it down the drain. I will recount her reasoning as best I can for you below:

Llanaber has a secular society. If it has a predominant religion it is Christianity, but we're pretty easy going on an individual's right to worship the God of their choice. We do have other faiths as well as Christians in the village as follows:

Those of the Druish persuasion (e.g. Solly Weinstein, Mrs. T's lawyer, amateur video maker and official village pervert) – they believe that anyone living on a sand dune should be persecuted.

The Catholics – they believe in the infallibility of the Pope, apologizing for the molestation of children, and spending their collection money on gold, glass topped cars, expensive lunches and settling pedophile lawsuits out of court.

The Muslims – No one dare say anything about them in case the tiny minority of zealots in their ranks comes looking for you.

Foggists – this is an unusual religion at the core of which is the worship of Llanaber's perpetual fog. They see it as the manifestation of the essential spirit of mankind, i.e. thick and dull.

We all live in tolerance and harmony. However, if the Incas started turning up and suddenly there were sun-worshippers entering the mix, then the equilibrium would be upset. There would be disharmony. Noses would be put 'out of joint.' It may even end in war!

"In addition to which," she concluded, "I have it on very good authority that Mexicans are all rapists and murderers. What's more they're all drug dealers, and we can't have that sort of thing in the village. It would upset the official village pusher, 'Iolo the Dope,' and we don't want that addle-brained idiot putting his prices up again."

I could not argue with her logic. I set to work immediately designing a suitable system that could be put in place quickly to ban Incas from the village pro-tem. I say pro-tem because, as with Mr. Trump in the US, any such ban would need to be tested for its legality through the courts. This is not an easy thing to do. Justice is meted out in our village by a peripatetic judge, Lord Justice Brown-Envelope. He only visits the village courts once every ten years, and he isn't due for another eight.

But in the interim, I have prepared a poster campaign. This consists of three large posters with black lettering on a scarlet background for maximum impact. The posters are to be pasted onto three billboards on the road into the village. I have taken a great deal of care not to offend any tribe, religion, creed, color, gender or sexual preference in the construction of the message. The wording will be in a sequence, so anyone driving into the village would read the message as below:

"Incas not welcome."

"Go away!"

"I said GO AWAY!"

I would never profess to be a great marketer, but I think this simple message tells the story.

On reflection I have to admit that for once Mrs. T got it spot on. We don't want the religious harmony of the village disrupted by interlopers with a religion alien to those with which we are familiar. We are a simple people. We fear the unknown. We fear what we do not understand. The arrival in the village of a tribe of sun-worshippers that has been extinct for over four hundred years would put a strain on us all, and put at risk the bonhomie that exists between the different religions currently.

That said, the Druids don't exactly get along with the Travelers (who are Muslims, I think). Also, while we pretend otherwise, not many of us really like the Druids. They're a big headed lot with too much money, and are forever trying to twist our arms to be nasty to the Travelers and forcing us to turn a blind eye when they beat up the Travelers' kids. And the Catholics are a funny lot. You have to tell their priest all the bad stuff you've done so he can blackmail you. I'm not that keen on the Christians either, if I'm honest. They're a toothless bunch that pay themselves too much and are always at the front of the queue when there's a disaster, mouthing off as if they 'understood' why it happened.

In truth the only religion in the village I've got any time for is the Foggists. I've no idea what they do, though. They just dress up in long robes and walk out on the beach into the fog. They then make a lot of grunting noises, and when they come back out of the fog they're all wearing each other's clothes and looking tired but satisfied.

I may join. So, the last thing I want is Incas turning up and hacking them off!

That's it for now. Cheerio!

'TRUMP' STYLE INFLATABLE PROTEST NEAR MISS IN LLANABER

Protesters are planning to fly a huge inflatable baby Trump over London (TrumpBabyUK/Twitter)

I have often been confused by the drivel that dribbles from my esteemed leader, Mrs. Dorothy 'Binky' Trim's mouth. However, I think today a new high (or is it low?) was reached.

It appeared that the old bat had somehow got wind of the anti-Trump demonstrations that are planned with the quiet, self-effacing megalomaniac visits the UK on July 13 for bi-lateral talks with the UK's corresponding idiot, Theresa 'weak and unstable' May.

Many demonstrations are planned in the UK to let the cheese-ball headed comb-over brainiac and anorexia denier

Trump know some people are not exactly enamored of the narcissistic buffoon.

Why would this be of interest to our own idiot leader here in Llanaber?

(I hear you cry).

Let me recount events exactly as they happened.

I was having a quiet nap in my office when Mrs. Trim suddenly burst in, kicked my legs off my desk and slapped a newspaper down. She thrust her arm out and pointed at a picture on the front page and bellowed, "I found this in the bin outside. What are you doing about it?"

I looked at the article. The headline read:

"LONDON — A 20-foot-tall inflatable orange baby with the face of President Donald Trump could float over Britain's parliament next month, one of many acts of protest planned to coincide with Trump's first visit to the U.K. since taking office."

The photo that appeared to have so vexed Mrs. Trim is NOT reproduced for you below. It would give small children nightmares.

I asked the obvious stupid question, "What do you want me to do about it?"

"I WANT MY OWN! GET OFF YOUR LAZY BUTT AND GET IT SORTED!" she bellowed before crashing back out of my office slamming the door behind her.

I was given no opportunity to ask her how or even why the deranged old basket case would want such a thing, i.e. an inflatable grotesque effigy of herself.

In previous instances when my esteemed leader has asked for the insane, the zany, or the downright illegal, I've played safe and put her request 'on the record,' just in case the parish council is ever subjected to the scrutiny of 'a higher authority' i.e. those sticky beak, nosey, interfering troublemakers from the Gwynedd council auditor's office.

I'm nothing if not a loyal servant to both my office as village Foreign Secretary and to the incumbent parish council leader. I put loyalty above all my other attributes.

However, it's always both prudent and reassuring to have ones butt well and truly covered by a paper trail leading from Mrs. Trim's instructions via my desk to whatever the debacle is, to show beyond a shadow of a doubt it was 'all her fault.'

It also helps to make clear what the likely consequences are for whatever ridiculous project is undertaken.

I set about clarifying her instructions in the form of an email as follows:

"To: Binky (we dispense with the formal when emailing each other)

From: David

Date: June 27 2018

Subject: A 20ft high inflatable effigy of Dorothy 'Binky' Trim – Acquisition of, and deployment details.

Dear Binky,

Confirming your instruction that I will set about the acquisition of the above.

As you left my office without giving me more precise information, I will be carrying out the task as follows:

1.   Review the village hospital's budget to the tune of $6,500: I understand the one of Trump was crowd-funded to this value.

N.B. Expect complaints from Dr. Mengele (The boss of the hospital). He is already performing operations by candlelight as there are insufficient funds left in the budget to pay the hospital's electricity bill. Also he now can't afford to have the village scalpel sharpened. Further, he has had to have the length of all crutches shortened by two feet to save on wood.

2.   Commissioning an artisan to create the balloon: To this end I have sent photographs of yourself in various

'poses' to the village balloon expert, 'Beppo, the Sad-Faced Clown.' As you know he specializes in bending balloons into various shapes as part of his cabaret act. As some of these are obscene, I have given him specific instructions to 'keep it clean.' He has studied the brief and is confident he can 'knock something up' from an old bouncy castle he has lining his dog's kennel.

3.   Ordering a delivery of helium for the balloon's inflation: As you know the village has no storage tank for Helium, so I have asked that protem, i.e. until the balloon is ready, the gas is stored in black plastic refuse sacks tied at the neck and kept upside down till required. The Helium supplier, 'Dai the Gas' estimates we will need 9,000 black bin liners. There is insufficient storage space available anywhere in the village so I've made provisions that the bags are nailed onto the rugby pitch once filled. As the season's fixtures have all been completed, the field will be standing there doing nothing till September. I have checked the weather forecast for the period up to the date of commissioning the balloon. The weather is as follows: Fog.

The estimated completion date for this project is July 13. Where do you want me to have the inflated finished article tethered?
Best,
David"

I sat back in my chair and pressed the 'send' button satisfied that I had not only correctly interpreted her requirements, followed her instructions to the letter but also sufficiently covered my exposed private parts should at a future date 'awkward questions be asked.' There could be no ambiguity should the 'incompetence police' from Gwynedd headquarters pounce in one of their 'dawn raids.' It was now all in black and white and 'on the record.'

So, I was completely mystified when moments after sending the email, Mrs. T came crashing into my office and lifted me from my chair by my neck.

"You complete and utter MORON!" she yelled, "I meant the newspaper, not the fecking balloon!"

I had misunderstood, got it wrong, messed up, failed the most basic of numpty intelligence tests. It was so obvious when she pointed out my (in my mind perfectly understandable) massive blooper.

Let me explain.

There are no newspapers in Llanaber. Our source of news from the outside world is restricted to the parish council ticker tape news feed and the occasional TV program on the rare occasions when the perpetual fog lifts. Newspaper deliveries only get as far as Druidellau. From there arrangements have been set in place to have newsprint 'onwardly moved' using newspaper delivery boys. These are drawn from the ranks of the Travelers' kids. However, as soon as they set off for Llanaber, the Druids' henchmen set their devil dogs on them, usually tearing both the newspapers and the delivery boys to shreds.

So, when Mrs. T came across an ACTUAL newspaper in the village, she quite rightly assumed that a new delivery route had been set up. As such she was not asking for a giant inflatable effigy of herself, but for me to ensure she gets her own personal copy of a daily newspaper.

I had erred, I know, and I worked hard to re-establish my credentials as a competent professional in the eyes of my superior. A quick investigation soon discovered that the newspaper Mrs. T had found in the bin had been dumped there by an American tourist passing through the village, the said item having been bought in Druidellau earlier that morning. No new arrangements for daily newspaper deliveries were in place.

Mrs. T gave me the worst tongue lashing I have ever had in my career.

I took my medicine like a man.

As I left her office, belittled and humiliated, my ears still ringing from her verbal jaw-bashing, I could not help but smile. Better the yelling than a twenty-foot-high blimp of that fat old cow hovering over the village for the foreseeable future, eh?

That's it for now.

Cheerio!

NEW SUPREME COURT APPOINTMENT SPELLS DIRE PROSPECTS FOR DEMOCRACY

I have a confession to make. Today I bunked off work for half an hour. The stress of the job of being parish Foreign Secretary of late has become almost intolerable. My esteemed leader, the boss of the parish council, Mrs. Dorothy 'Binky' Trim is growing more insane by the day. Each meeting I have with the old bat is like stepping into Caligula's office holding a sign saying 'I Hate Your Horse.'

I had a nerve jangling session with her this morning in which she demanded that all copies of Madeleine Albright's new book about Fascism had to be burnt and the ashes thrown into the enormous sink hole in the high street, including all the e-copies! I asked her if she had actually read the thing, bearing in mind the village has neither a book shop, a library or internet access. She replied in the negative but added, "But I know it criticizes the most wonderful man in the world (the Duck), and I won't have the village contaminated with her filth."

I told her I would 'get right on it' and slipped out of her office. I could take no more. I went out the back door of the parish council building and headed for the sea front (at least I thought I did. The perpetual fog was down so I could have been heading in the wrong direction). Anyway, I was walking through the swirling fog lamenting my woes when who should I bump into (literally – the fog was especially thick) than the official village gossip, old Mrs. Winfrey. She grabbed me by the collar in a vain attempt to stop herself from toppling over and whispered in my ear as she tumbled, "Have you heard the latest?"

She then went on to tell me one of her usual conflated stories, most of which was garbage. I repeat verbatim what the old girl hissed in my ear as her massive bulk inexorably sank to the ground:

"Donald Trump is working with the Jurassic Park people to genetically recreate Adolf Hitler and Atilla the Hun, so he can make them fight each other for the job of the next Supreme Court judge when John F Kennedy retires."

I rather ungentlemanly left the old girl lying there in the mud and fog, struggling to raise her massive carcass back to the vertical, and ran back to the office. I had to get to the news feed ticker tape room ahead of Mrs. T. If she saw what I thought the actual piece of news was likely to be, it would spell big trouble for the village.

I feared that the news clip would be about Judge Anthony Kennedy announcing his retirement, and that the baldy comb-over and anorexia denier Trump would be lining up an 'ultra-right winger' for the Supreme Court team. This would determine the future of the US for decades to come. America would lurch even further to the right. The age of US 'red neck' supremacy would be upon us.

But why should this bother me so far away here in Llanaber? (I hear you cry).

Lord Justice Brown-Envelope!

Justice is dispensed in the village once every ten years by the above named peripatetic judge. He is a hundred and six years old and is due to either retire or be embalmed any day now. If Mrs. Trim sees that 'the Duck' can manipulate the justice system to ensure his personal choice of Supreme Court judge gets the post, then she'll do likewise here.

Imagine it, dear reader, Mrs. T with her hand up the back of the ventriloquist's dummy she would put in charge of dishing out justice in the village. It would be yet another giant stride towards her ambition to make Llanaber her totalitarian state, her thiefdom, her very own kleptocracy.

Who in Llanaber would be the puppet of which Mrs. T would pull the strings? (I hear you ask again).

It would undoubtedly be none other than her blubby-hubby Mr. Leonard Arbuthnot Trim.

Yes, it would be him I have no doubt about it. She would give him the job for the following reason:

He has a low level 'O' certificate in Business Law (Packaging & Labelling).

There!

That's it.

The truth is out.

To everyone in the village, Leonard is considered a brainless imbecile and professional glutton that couldn't think his way out of a bag of crisps. The fact is, relative to everyone else in the village*, he is by comparison a
'legal eagle.'

I have seen his 'official file.'

Late one night after a parish council meeting, I fell asleep on 'the can' in the restroom and accidentally got locked in the building overnight. For the want of something better to do I snuck into the 'human resources' office and read every one of Mrs. Trim's 'secret dossiers.' (She likes to keep the dirt on all her staff in case she needs to twist the occasional bollock now and then to ensure she gets her own way).

It was there I discovered that, despite the 'dumb as a brick' facade, Leonard actually had been to school. Further, he was a veritable expert when it came to the legal complexities of yogurt pot labelling, and the intricacies of cigarette carton legislation. He's a natural. His certificate confirmed his pass was of the highest grade, A1.

*Obviously, Mrs. Trim's personal lawyer and village pervert, Solly Weinstein (no relation) is the most qualified in legal matters but he would be prohibited from holding such high office as he has a criminal record. He was given three months community service (cleaning the garbage from around the top of the sink hole) for measuring the village maidens' belly buttons without their prior consent.

When I arrived back at the parish council building my heart sank. Mrs. T was in my office clutching a string of ticker tape in her hand and wearing what I can only describe as a nauseating grin on her face. I did not need to read the news clip. I instinctively knew what it was. She looked at me with a sick-making sneer on her face and said, "If he can get away with it, then so can I."

She turned on her heels and walked out of my office, cackling insanely.

I want no part of any administration that would so manipulate justice as to bring about a right wing fascist totalitarian state to be plundered for the sole benefit of one individual and her (or his) immediate family and friends.

It is too much.

It is intolerable.

I cannot support living in a society so bent out of shape that the very foundation of democracy, the justice system, is controlled at the whim of a despot.

As I write, I have in front of me an envelope. In this is a single sheet of paper. It is a letter addressed to Mrs. Dorothy 'Binky' Trim, and confirms my resignation as Llanaber parish council Foreign Secretary.

I will move to Spanibont and join the rowdies. Better to live outside the law than be subjugated by it.

Besides, they've got a pub in Spanibont, the 'Abandon All Hope.' The best Llanaber can boast is 'Trevor the Trots' Trattoria, and their beer's shit.

That's it… possibly forever.

Cheerio!